Once Robert had said something about love

About loving her. She remembered the words and yet she didn't. Was it that she had wanted to hear him say it? Had she wanted it so badly that she hallucinated? Or had he said them and then immediately regretted it?

Everything had been so out of kilter. Their lives had been turned upside down. Intimacies were accepted as normalcy. They had kissed, they had held each other . . . Did that mean anything now?

Anne shivered in the warmth. She needed him, she wanted him, she loved him. But possibly she was the type of person who would never receive love in return. Through no fault of her own was she meant to be solitary? From childhood on was she never destined to find the hidden treasures of love and warmth and caring?

ABOUT THE AUTHOR

Ginger Chambers gets story ideas from a variety of sources. Sometimes she starts with a specific character in mind, puts the person in a situation and watches as the action starts to evolve. Such was the case with *Call My Name Softly*, in which she once again returns to an action-oriented, mysterious plot like the one she used in *Firefly in the Night*. A native of Texas, Ginger makes her home in northern California with her husband and two teenagers.

Books by Ginger Chambers

HARLEQUIN AMERICAN ROMANCE

Don't miss any of our special offers. Write to us at the following address for information on our newest releases.

Harlequin Reader Service
901 Fuhrmann Blvd., P.O. Box 1397, Buffalo, NY 14240
Canadian address: P.O. Box 603,
Fort Erie, Ont. L2A 5X3

Call My Name Softly
Ginger Chambers

Harlequin Books

TORONTO • NEW YORK • LONDON
AMSTERDAM • PARIS • SYDNEY • HAMBURG
STOCKHOLM • ATHENS • TOKYO • MILAN

Published July 1988

First printing May 1988

ISBN 0-373-16254-5

Prologue

"Mr. Foreman, have you reached a verdict?"

The words rang hollowly in the hushed courtroom. All eyes were riveted on the head juror, the one person in twelve who was standing.

Anne Reynolds sat with her hands tightly locked, her heart hammering wildly in her chest. She felt the tension of the people around her almost as keenly as she felt her own.

"Yes, we have, your honor," came the reply.

"Then would you please give it to the bailiff."

With practiced ease the officer moved to collect the sealed envelope that held the decision. His return to the station of the clerk was accomplished just as slowly.

The clerk then took the envelope to the judge who opened it, read it and handed it back to be read aloud.

The clerk, his voice a gruff rumble of authority, went through a ritual deliverance of place and statute before divulging the decision: "...find the defendants *guilty*..."

His words continued, but pandemonium broke loose in the crowded room. Shocked outbursts of protest blended with heartrending cries from members of the defendants' families, while members of the news media—anxious to be first with the breaking story—pushed and shoved their way into the hallway outside where other reporters, who could not cram into the courtroom, blocked the way.

For the moment Anne couldn't move. It was almost as if her body no longer belonged to her. She was a part of it but she wasn't in command.

The judge rapped his gavel, calling for order.

The two defendants, both men in their late fifties, sat in stunned disbelief. Their lawyers conferred, and then leaned close to offer reassurance. Quick incisive hand motions accompanied their muted words.

Finally the judge regained control, and asked if the counselors wished to have the jury polled. Of course the defense attorneys did, but the outcome remained the same; and soon the judge was ordering the dismissal of the jury, setting a time for sentencing and standing up to leave the bench—his role in the nightmare that had torn at the heart of one small town and captured the interest of a nation finished for the moment.

As soon as the judge stepped down from his exalted position, the noise level again increased. People couldn't believe what had happened.

Anne heard their voices, felt the censure of their eyes. She wanted to sink lower in her seat, to protect herself, but pride wouldn't let her go to that extreme. She had done nothing wrong.

The two men sitting on either side of her stood up. She got to her feet as well.

"Well, that's done," one said. He didn't sound particularly pleased.

"Yes," replied the other.

Together the three of them had been the prosecution's main witnesses: the two FBI agents who had investigated the case, and herself, the person who had broken the silence.

The taller of the two men reached out to shake Anne's hand. "Miss Reynolds, I believe you know you have the government's gratitude. I want to give you mine, too. I know it's not been easy for you."

"No..." Anne replied. His touch was cool when she needed warmth. The second man made no attempt to reach out to her.

Anne knew more eyes had come to rest on them. She felt resentment break against her like a crushing wave.

When the prosecutor started to move toward them with a wide, triumphant smile on his rather homely face, it was more than she could bear. Murmuring a muffled excuse, she moved past the men into the aisle.

Sudden silence greeted her arrival. People stood in the way, forcing her to choose between either pushing past them or halting.

Anne *had* to get out of the room. A cold film of perspiration bathed her body as she twisted past rigid bodies bearing faces that had once smiled at her in greeting and now looked upon her with hate.

She was almost to the door when a rough hand caught her arm and drew her around. Emily Thompson's malevolent features thrust close as she hissed, "I hope you don't think people will forget this. Two good men . . . and look what you've done to them."

Anne tried to pull away. "They did it to themselves, Emily."

"No one believes that. No one believes *you*!"

"The jury did."

"The jury was *wrong*." The woman took a breath. "Just don't think you're going to be able to come back to Overton and pretend that this didn't happen. If you want a helpful hint, go back to your house, get your things together and leave town."

"Are you threatening me?" Anne demanded. People were moving out of the courtroom now. She was being jostled, probably on purpose.

"I'm not threatening, I'm telling. We have ways of dealing with traitors."

"I'm not the traitor, *they* are!"

"So you say. If I were you I'd listen to what I'm telling you . . . or things might get messy."

"I'm not going to leave!" Anne swore.

"Then be prepared to pay the price."

Anne slapped the woman's hand away and spun around. She wanted to run. But there were too many people in the way. Emotion clogged her throat, yet she would not cry. Not now. Not in front of them. If she did, they might think that they had won.

"Liar," she heard someone hiss.

"Busybody!" someone else accused.

As they moved en masse into the hall outside the courtroom, a member of the media spotted her and she was soon surrounded by microphones and bright lights, cut off from the others, left to stand alone to face the barrage of questions.

"Bitch!" The softly worded accusation drifted through a break in the questioning, giving a new direction to the media's curiosity.

She didn't seem a very popular figure... did the people of Overton resent what she had done? Was there any truth to the rumor that Kinkaid Systems was going to shut down because of what had occurred?

The taller FBI agent came to her aid, his professional demeanor drawing their attention. The questioning immediately centered on him, allowing Anne to slip away.

She left the courthouse by a side door and hurried to her car. She had parked it in a secluded area, hoping that it wouldn't be noticed, that *she* wouldn't be noticed when she came back to claim it.

But as she drew near, she saw that someone had gotten there before her. All four tires were flat, her radio antenna had been broken off, and her windshield wipers had been bent backward in an arc—they looked like the wings of a broken bird, no longer useful, no longer alive.

Automatically, she searched the area around her, but she saw no one. The vandal had disappeared. He had left a calling card, though: a note. It was taped to the handle of one door.

Don't come back to Overton. If you do, you'll only get worse!

Anne crushed the note in trembling anger. She *would* go back. She wouldn't allow herself to be intimidated. Not by anyone!

A car careered around the corner, its tires screaming. As it went by, its passengers yelled obscenities and someone hurled a rock.

The rock hit the car's fender close to Anne's hand, making her jump. Her reaction gained nasty laughter.

When the car was gone, Anne drew a shaky breath, tears wanting very badly to fall.

However, a group of people suddenly appeared on the sidewalk at the corner and Anne recognized them as more residents of Overton. Panic-stricken, she wanted to turn, to hide in the tall bushes at her side. But it was too late. They had seen her.

Acting quickly, she jumped into her car, relocking the door behind her. The vehicle might not be drivable, but it did offer some form of protection.

Only this time no one looked at her. As they silently walked past, they kept their gazes fixed firmly on the sidewalk ahead.

Anne remained perfectly still...waiting. Then, when she saw that they, too, were gone, she released her long pent-up breath. For the moment she was safe. For *this* moment.

Then a car backfired some distance down the street.

Her first instinct was to duck.

Chapter One

Suddenly, with a gasp, Anne sat up, her body coiled for flight. *If she didn't escape, the people would . . .*

Seconds passed, seconds in which her surroundings slowly registered on her consciousness, seconds in which she realized that she had no need to run now, no need to fear what the next moment might bring. She was far from Overton, far from the hateful acts that had wounded her so deeply. But telling herself that and making her body believe it were two different things. Her heart continued to flutter as she put a trembling hand to her mouth. A terrified scream still hovered on her lips.

Finally, she slumped back against the soft cushion of the lounge chair and covered her eyes with her arm. A tear escaped into her hair; its warmth, along with its solace, invited others to follow. She had been doing a lot of crying recently.

In the end, Overton had won. The people hadn't wanted her there and they had made their feelings abundantly clear.

But it was hard to give up a home. Hard to give up the claim of her right to live there.

Anne allowed herself a moment of self-pity. She needed it. She had *earned* it.

Then a sound—based in reality, not from a dream—caused her to sit up again with a start. The sound repeated.

Anne shot a glance at the sliding glass door. She could be inside within three seconds. She could be locked in the house . . . safe!

But for how much longer could she continue to run? A week? A month? A year? At some point she had to stop.

This *wasn't* Overton.

She pushed unsteadily to her feet, wiping away the traces of tears as she moved to the deck railing. The hot California sun beat down on her head at the same time as the ocean breeze cooled her skin.

Her eyes swept over the pool-and-patio area of the level below and she saw nothing unusual. Her gaze then switched to the unkempt land on either side of the property.

Again, she saw nothing; until, on the left, a movement caught her attention. It was a child! Of no more than five or six. He was standing outside the low ornamental fence, peering up at her from beneath a thatch of pale blond hair.

As she watched, he bent to pick up a small stone. Then he flashed a quick grin as he lobbed it into the air.

Anne blinked in surprise, following its trajectory into the pool. Several other small stones were already there.

Her grip tightened on the railing. She had rented this beach house because of its isolation. Where had *he* come from?

"Don't do that! Go away!" she ordered.

The child was not swayed by her directive. As she watched, he hurled another stone into the pool, then had the nerve to giggle.

Under other circumstances Anne's patience would have been longer. But she had been through so much lately—had suffered too many acts of related vandalism. To the child, this was probably just a game. But to her frayed nerves...

"Do you live around here?" she asked in as steady a tone as she could muster. "What's your name?"

The child didn't answer.

Anne tried to remain calm. "Would you at least tell me why you're doing this? You do *have* a reason..."

Reasons. Everyone had reasons. The good people of Overton certainly thought they did. That was why they had turned from warm, friendly people into vigilantes, protecting their own—or more correctly, gaining revenge for their own. The two men she had testified against were products of the town. Each was active in the community; their parents and grandparents had roots in the area! *She* was the newcomer in town; she had only lived there for two years. When sides were taken, no one had lined up with her, not even the people she had thought to be her friends. Whether through conviction or through their fear of being shunned, no one had defended her.

That the men had betrayed a sacred trust seemed to mean little. What counted was jobs, or rather the loss of jobs. Kinkaid Systems had been the largest employer in the area. Overton's economy revolved around it and the prestige it brought to their community. And they blamed her for its demise.

A shaft of impotent anger burned through Anne's soul and she gave in to the need to strike back. "You little brat!" she shouted. "If you do that again, you're going to regret it! I'll come down there and find your parents. I'll tell them what you've done. What you—"

Anne stopped when she saw that her anger was getting his attention. His eyes had shadowed with misgiving and he had begun to back away. At first, neither saw the danger lying in wait, and when Anne did see it, it was too late. She only had time to begin a cry of warning when the child tripped over a large outcropping of exposed roots and began to tumble down the embankment. His sharp cry of fear blended with hers until it suddenly ended.

Anne was paralyzed, stunned. She couldn't believe what had happened. One moment she was there alone; the next she was not. And now the child... She shook herself free of shock and raced downstairs and across the patio, not hesitating to hop across the short fence.

On the other side the ground was rough and steeply banked to the shoreline. She slid more than she stepped until she was at the bottom. The child was at its base, lying still. Lying very still.

Gone were all thoughts of herself, of the difficulties she had experienced. She had been annoyed with the child, but she didn't want him to be hurt! She fell to her knees at his side and tried to remember the rudiments of first aid. Should she touch him—turn him over? Or would it be best to leave him alone and get help?

The boy ended the debate for her. Uttering a muffled little groan, he shifted position and lifted his head. Wounded blue eyes fluttered open to look at her.

Anne swallowed tightly. Thank God! At least he was alive!

"Honey...sweetheart..." she said softly. "Are you all right? Does anything hurt?"

"My knees," he moaned.

"Can you turn the rest of the way over?" She tried to keep the uncertainty out of her voice. Her entire body felt boneless.

"I think so."

Anne forced an encouraging smile as he put action to his words.

"Just lie still for a minute now, okay?" She ran shaking hands over his limbs, unsure of exactly what she was looking for: swelling, a bone out of line. She had never done this before. She made her smile bright when she finished. "Well, I think you're still in one piece."

His small hands went to his knees, where blood was pooling in the deep scratches. "I want my daddy! I want my mommy!"

"I know you do, honey." Anne sat back on her heels. She looked in both directions down the lonely beach. There was nothing to be seen but jagged outcroppings of rock. "You live around here?" she asked.

The boy gave a halfhearted nod.

Anne tilted her gaze toward what could be seen of her rental house, a section of its deck and roof. It was a long way up. Her attention returned to the boy. He would have to be carried. He was moving now, talking, but she couldn't be sure that he wasn't more seriously hurt. "My name is Anne," she offered, as much to take his mind off his pain as to introduce herself. "What's yours?"

All the impudence had left the child. He answered promptly, if a little shyly, "Jamie."

She smiled. "Well, Jamie. We're going to have to get back up this hill. When I lean forward, I want you to wrap your arms around my neck. I'm going to carry you."

"I'm not a baby!" he quickly defended.

"Oh, I know that," she said. "But since your knees are hurt, it will be hard for you to climb."

The boy's attention returned to his wounds. Tears welled in his eyes. "I want my daddy now!"

"I'll get him for you," Anne promised. "But first we have to find a telephone... and it's up there." She pointed up the hill again.

He bit his bottom lip. It still managed to tremble.

Anne didn't waste any more time. She leaned forward, clasped him under his knees and pushed to her feet. His thin arms came out to wrap around her neck in a hold a wrestler would have found difficult to break.

"Everything will be fine. You'll see," she tried to reassure him.

The boy remained silent and they started the climb. Anne was in fairly good condition—she exercised regularly—but nothing had prepared her for the weight of the child. He looked thin, yet it was all she could do to gain the top of the embankment. She was puffing and the color in her cheeks was high by the time they arrived at the house.

She placed the boy on a comfortable chair and slid to a seat on the floor beside him. Several seconds passed before she asked, "Do you know your phone number?"

The boy shook his head.

"What about your address?"

Again the blond head shook.

Anne frowned. "What's your father's name then? You do know that, don't you?"

Jamie nodded with exaggerated motion, seemingly relieved that he could satisfy at least one of her demands. "His name's Robert."

Noting his relief, Anne softened the edge that had crept into her tone. "What's your last name?" The fact that his parents were lax in seeing that he learned the essentials was not the boy's fault.

"Singleton." Jamie looked at his knees and sniffed.

Anne leaned forward to examine his wounds. She might not know what to do for a head injury, but she did for a cut.

Once she had his knees cleaned and antiseptic applied, an operation he took bravely, she found the area telephone booklet and looked inside. Yet as many times as she searched through the names, she found no Robert Singleton listed.

"Your father's name *is* Robert Singleton, isn't it, Jamie?"

He nodded.

She was going through the list once again when she felt the child's eyes resting on her. Her gaze lifted to meet his and after a moment she asked, "Would a bowl of ice cream help?'' She didn't know whether eating so soon after such an experience would be good for him, but it was the only thing she could think to do.

He nodded solemnly.

Anne excused herself. A short time later she returned, and the child accepted the vanilla ice cream with a soft ''Thank you.'' Anne watched as he dug into the frozen dessert. When he was done, she was just starting to ask if he would like more, when through the open door she heard the far-off sound of a man's voice calling someone's name. It came from the shoreline. She stepped closer and listened. The name was repeated and this time she recognized it as Jamie's.

Jamie heard the call as well and cried, ''Daddy!'' as he tried to hop to his feet. But his knees hurt so badly when he straightened that he almost crumpled to the floor.

''No, you stay there,'' Anne said quickly, helping him back to the chair. ''I'll bring your father to you.''

For once, Jamie did as he was told.

When she stepped outside, Anne heard that the man was much nearer; he must have been jogging along the narrow beach while he called. She leaned over the deck railing and raised her voice. ''Hello! Up here!''

There was no repeat of the name and for a moment only the assault of the surf on the sand could be heard. Then came a questioning ''Where are are you? I don't see you!''

''There's a trail of sorts,'' she shouted. Then she waited. Finally a man's form emerged close to the fence. As he straightened, she gave him a lightning-quick assessment. He was tall, with a long, lean body that spoke of a comfortable fitness, and his hair was blond, of a shade only slightly darker than Jamie's.

At first he didn't see her. He looked all around the patio area surrounding the pool before glancing up. Finally Anne received the full force of his gaze. The son's eyes were an unusual light blue, but the father's nearly identical shade was even more striking because of the deep tan of his skin. The contrast was startling in its intensity.

"Hello, there!" he said, breaking into a slow smile. "I don't suppose you've seen a little boy about so high—" he measured Jamie's size with his hand a distance from the ground "—playing around here, have you?"

How could he be so casual? Anne wondered. Didn't he care what happened to his son?

"I have," she answered coolly.

The man's smile widened. "Great. Where?"

"In the beginning he was throwing rocks into my pool."

"Sounds just like him," the man returned, unfazed.

Anne blinked. "I asked him not to."

"Did it do any good?"

"No."

"I didn't think so."

Anne stared at him, momentarily at a loss for words. If someone had told *her* father that she had done such a thing, he wouldn't have taken the situation so calmly, or with such tolerant amusement. It was almost as if this man approved! "And that doesn't bother you?" she challenged.

"He's only five."

"That's no excuse. He should be taught."

"He *has* been taught. Things just don't always take right away with kids."

Anne knew that she shouldn't get involved any further. Let the man come in, collect his son and get out. But not listening to instinct, she said frostily, "I hope you don't mean ever."

The smile came again. "He'll learn."

"By the school of hard knocks, I suppose?"

The man shrugged and Anne's mouth tightened. "Well, he's had his hard knock, at least his one for today. And I'd advise you to keep a better eye on him in the future. Next time it could be much worse."

The man's body instantly stiffened. "What are you saying?" he demanded.

"I'm saying that he's had a fall. He was up here by the fence, tripped on a root and fell down the embankment."

Without waiting for her to finish, the man vaulted over the fence and sprinted to the base of the stairs.

"Where is he?" he asked, none of the previous laid-back good humor remaining in his tone.

"In there," she motioned through the open doorway. As he rushed unceremoniously into the house, she quickly followed suit. "His knees were hurt so I cleaned them. I would have called, but I couldn't find your name in the telephone book."

The man gave no indication that he had heard her as he stopped to look down at his son. Jamie hung his head—not the reaction Anne expected.

Some of the father's tension faded as he continued to look at him. "You were supposed to be taking a nap. How'd you get out? The window?"

Jamie sniffed and nodded.

"Your mother said you were to have a nap each day."

"Don't like naps," Jamie returned.

The man sighed and eased himself onto one knee. "I seem to remember when I was five I didn't much care for naps either. But your mom wants you to have them." He paused. "Maybe when we go back we'll have a little talk with her and see if she doesn't think that you're getting old enough to skip one once in a while. What do you think?"

"All right!" Jamie replied, and a great, huge grin split his young face.

"Now," Robert Singleton leaned forward to examine his son more closely, "look at me for a minute."

Jamie did as he was asked, trying to stay still, trying to keep his gaze on his father and away from Anne who was standing in the background.

When he finished that part of the examination, the man checked the boy's pulse and felt around on him a bit before turning his attention to his knees.

"Hurt a lot?" he asked.

"A little bit," Jamie admitted.

"The lady did a good job." The man glanced at her.

"Her name's Anne," Jamie contributed. "She gave me ice cream!"

Anne was surprised that the boy remembered her name, especially considering the circumstances under which he had received it. "Shouldn't he be checked by a doctor?'' she suggested. ''He was unconscious when I found him.''

''He was probably just dazed. You took quite a fall, didn't you, sport?''

Jamie nodded.

''If he were my child—'' she started to say, only to be interrupted.

''But he's not,'' Robert Singleton said sharply.

Anne shut up, irritated by his breach of etiquette. His child had been harassing her. She had been under no obligation to help him—except for the obligations of common humanity, which she was not prepared to overlook.

Robert Singleton seemed to sense her thoughts and relaxed his aggressive stance. ''I've had training as a paramedic,'' he explained. ''I know what I'm doing. I don't see any signs of trouble, but I'll watch him. Is that all right with you?''

''Perfectly,'' Anne returned. All she wanted was for them to leave.

The man took a deep breath. ''Look, I appreciate what you did for my son. I'm sorry he gave you any trouble. Jamie, apologize to the lady for throwing rocks in her pool.''

''Her name's Anne,'' Jamie repeated. Then, under his father's direct gaze, he ducked his head and mumbled, ''I'm sorry.''

''And I apologize for the fright you must have had. It wasn't my idea for this to happen, though. And I doubt that it was Jamie's. It was just an accident.''

''One that could have been prevented,'' she retorted coolly.

"You mean you should have had the root removed?"

Anne stared at him. "This isn't my home. I'm just renting it."

"I'm renting mine for the month. That's why you couldn't find me in the phone book. We're neighbors. The place where Jamie and I are staying is just around the bend...Seal Cove, I think it's called."

Anne schooled her features to show no expression. Her idea of isolation and the real estate agent's were worlds apart.

The man turned to his son. "Are you ready to go home?" At the boy's nod, he bent to lift him. "I hope you don't mind if we use the back way again. We can get to our place by the road, but it would take three times as long."

"Not at all," Anne replied. Anything to be rid of them!

She followed the two males onto the deck and had to stop short when Robert Singleton turned to face her.

"I want to thank you again," he said.

Anne shrugged. "I'd do the same for anyone."

She felt the electric-blue eyes move over her face and shifted position under the perusal.

"Are you here all alone?" he suddenly asked. When Anne automatically stiffened, a slow smile spread over his attractive features. "I only asked because I want you to know that if you *are* alone and you ever need anything, I'm just down the beach. I think these are the only two houses for miles around."

"I'll remember that," Anne murmured tightly. But she knew that she would never call on him for help. As far as she was concerned, this would be their first and last encounter. At the moment she'd had more than enough of people.

Chapter Two

Robert Singleton stood in the doorway of the little cottage nestled in a protected area of Seal Cove. A dark frown clouded his expression as his gaze swept the great expanse of Pacific Ocean that was practically at his doorstep. Today there was no bank of concealing fog in the distance. He could see all the way to the vanishing point, where the curvature of the earth sucked the blue water from view. In a fanciful way, he almost believed he could see to China, and to those countries beyond—India, Pakistan, Bangladesh—which had called him so strongly so many, and yet so few, years ago.

Had it only been five years? God, it seemed longer than that. So many things had happened: some good, some not so good, some terrifying. Sometimes he felt so old. Yet he was only thirty-five. Thirty-five going on fifty.

Jamie made a soft sound in his sleep in the room behind him. The child had escaped taking a nap earlier in the day, the operative word being escaped, and now he was paying for his exertion. He had fallen asleep on the couch in the middle of his favorite television program and not even the songs of the Cookie Monster could keep him from his slumber.

Robert's eyes remained on his son, watching as he resettled into a more comfortable position. His little mouth was open slightly, his lashes pale against his cheeks, his hair tousled...

Robert turned away from the sight, his heart twisting painfully inside his chest. In the past five years, he had reported on insurrections, massacres, an assassination attempt, political and moral unrest, and an invasion of a nearby country. His work for the news service had won him the respect of both his superiors and his peers because of his dedication.

In *his* five years, Jamie had grown from a tiny, squalling infant into the young boy that he was today.

Which was more important? Robert knew the answer and cursed the brash, selfish decision that had torn him from his son.

He made no excuses for himself, because there were none. He had worked for years toward a goal and had taken it when it was offered. But he had missed so much—only during most of that time he hadn't realized his loss. To his shame, he had thought his life to be full. He had friends; his work was exciting, interesting. And whenever he let himself remember his son, he told himself that the boy was much better off in the States. With his mother... with his mother's new husband... in a stable home. His change of feeling had been gradual. A nagging edge that he couldn't put a finger on at first.

Over time the excitement of his work had lost some of its luster. And he began to question his priorities.

Robert reached into his shirt pocket for a cigarette, but stopped himself. He was trying to cut down, if not stop entirely. He didn't want Jamie to see him smoke. If he could be nothing else, he didn't want to be a bad influence.

His son made another small sound and Robert stepped away from the door, closing it, shutting out the cool breeze that swirled into the room to run its chilly fingers over the sleeping form.

At one time, Jamie had counted last in his view of the world.

Now, for the child, he would do anything.

ANNE LAY IN WHAT HAD BECOME one of her favorite spots, beneath the shade of a wooden-slatted sun shelter where heavily scented wisteria blooms hung like clusters of ripening grapes. It reminded her of ancient Greece or Rome, where the gods of old had spent their time on earth.

Her lips curved into a sleepy smile. Several days had passed since her arrival and in that time she had begun to relax. There had been no acts of vandalism to mar her days—no rotten eggs broken on her front door, no unsigned messages that threatened retribution, no wanton destruction of the business she had worked so hard to build. In contrast, it seemed she had at last found peace. Occasionally she thought she heard voices and laughter coming from the direction of the cove, but she never saw the man or his son.

As she continued to lie still, her eyelids grew heavy, and her mind began to drift in that curiously light sensation entered just before sleep. Soon she would know nothing at all....

A childish whisper thrust its way into her consciousness. "She's sleeping, Daddy!"

"Just like Sleeping Beauty," a much more mature voice replied.

With fascinated curiosity, the child asked, "Are you gonna be like the prince and kiss her?"

At that Anne struggled to sit up, startled to complete wakefulness. Since she was near the pool, she was close to the two males who were standing outside the low fence.

Robert Singleton smiled slightly, as Anne quickly reached for a wrap to cover the skimpiness of her swimsuit.

"We didn't mean to startle you," he said, his son's small hand held in his.

"Hi, Anne!" Jamie piped in his high, clear voice.

Anne forced a smile as she attempted to push her arms through the gossamer material. "Hi, Jamie," she returned. Even under the best of circumstances, she had never enjoyed being caught unaware. She appreciated it even less now.

"We came to see if you'd like to have dinner with us!" Jamie exclaimed.

The boy's father smiled. "Well, we were going to lead up to it a *little* slower."

"Oh" was all Anne could think to say. She'd finally succeeded in settling the wrap around her body and was now running her fingers quickly through her hair.

"We also wanted to show you my knees!" Jamie exclaimed again. A lot of what Jamie said seemed to be exclaimed. He scrabbled over the fence and hurried to Anne's side. His father followed more slowly.

Anne dutifully examined first one proffered knee and then the next. "They certainly look better," she complimented, giving a tight smile.

"They're almost well," Jamie agreed.

Robert Singleton stood a short distance away. He had to squint against the brightness of the sun, but he had no trouble observing the woman. She was of average height and weight, but the way the balance was distributed on her body definitely did things for the swimsuit she was wearing—at least what he had seen of it before she finally succeeded in hiding behind the bright coverup. Long, shapely legs were still exposed, though, along with narrow ankles and delicately formed feet. Her chestnut hair curved forward on her cheeks as she listened to his son. Her profile was attractively drawn, as were her features. While he continued to scrutinize her, she darted a quick glance at him with eyes that were a light hazel. He hadn't noticed all that much about her the last time they met. He gave another slow smile that made her look away.

"Daddy says they'll be completely well soon," Jamie confided.

"I suppose we should formally introduce ourselves," his father said at last. "I'm Robert Singleton. This, as you know, is Jamie. And you're Anne—"

"Reynolds," she supplied, because she saw no other way around the moment.

He continued, "Now that we have that out of the way... would you like to have dinner with us this evening? Nothing formal. We thought we'd barbecue a few burgers down on the beach."

Anne barely let him finish. "No, I don't think so. Thank you, but—"

"Please?" Jamie intervened. "Daddy said you might not want to come, but I told him you would. I said I was sorry for what I did. I'll get the rocks out of your pool. I promise. And I won't do it again."

Anne met the boy's pleading gaze. "It's not that—"

"We've got plenty of meat and buns...and loads of chips. They're Jamie's favorite food next to ice cream."

The reference to the child's favorite food and the realization that she had inadvertently hit upon it after his accident passed only briefly over Anne's consciousness. "No, I can't. Really. I..."

"At least think about it," Robert Singleton urged. "If you decide you want to come, come. If you don't, don't. We're going to be down on the beach either way."

Jamie looked disappointed, but his father didn't give him time to make a further plea. The boy was scooped up to a playful position across the man's shoulder and transported across the fence. The last Anne saw of them was Jamie's face looking back at her, while his father carried him carefully down the embankment.

Anne remained motionless, as surprised by the abruptness of their departure as she had been by their arrival. Then she lay back on the lounge chair and reclaimed the book she had been reading earlier, opening it to the correct page. But when she tried to become involved in its complicated plot, she found that her mind wouldn't cooperate. Several undigested paragraphs later, she sighed and retagged her place. She couldn't get the child's face out of her mind. He had looked so serious when apologizing for throwing the rocks...and his was the first apology she had received in a very long time!

Anne stood up to move restlessly across the patio, trying to convince herself that she had done the right thing in turning down their invitation, especially since she didn't want to go. But contrarily, there was something very seductive about the invitation: she hadn't realized how much she missed human contact—nonjudgmental human contact—until now.

She paced the width of the patio, her peace once again disturbed.

"SHE'S HERE, DADDY! She's here!" Jamie's penetrating voice instantly wrecked Anne's attempt at casualness. The little boy raced along the water's edge until he reached her. Then, without warning, his thin arms wrapped around her skirt to hug her legs with surprising strength. His eyes were shining as he looked up at her. "I knew you'd come," he crowed triumphantly. He gave her legs another delighted hug before turning to skip happily at her side.

The boy's father was standing at a barbecue grill. "Just in time," he greeted. "Glad you could make it."

Anne instantly wished that she had listened to her first inclination. She should have stayed away. She definitely wasn't ready to socialize. Jamie was still skipping by her side, only now he was managing to do it in place. She cleared her throat. "But I'm not—"

Robert Singleton's eyes narrowed as he looked across at her. She felt rather than saw him frown.

"I hope you're hungry," he said, ignoring her half-stated denial as he expertly flipped meat patties onto a plate.

"I am!" Jamie answered. "I've been hungry for hours!"

"I know that, sport. You've been telling me every five minutes."

Jamie grinned, throwing Anne an impish look to which she tried to respond. Her instincts were telling her to hurry away from these people, from this place— that Robert Singleton and his son would only mean trouble for her.

"I think everything's ready here," Robert Singleton continued. "Jamie, why don't you find out what Anne would like to drink."

Jamie looked at her expectantly. "Do you want an orange soda?" he asked.

"We have more than just that," his father corrected.

"Yeah," the boy returned, "but orange soda is the best."

Robert shook his head in amused tolerance. "We do have other types," he said to Anne.

"An orange soda is fine. But really, I didn't mean to stay. I just came to... I was just out for a walk and..."

"So you're here now. Why don't you relax and have something to eat. You look as if you could use it."

Anne gave him a nervous glance and he smiled, causing her to smooth her palms against the soft material of her skirt.

"Make that three, Jamie. And be careful how you go. Especially on the stairs."

Jamie whirled around to scamper up the gentle incline that led to the cottage positioned a short distance away.

Robert checked his son's progress before turning his attention back to Anne. "If you want to go ahead and make your burger, the fixings are over there." He pointed to a small table that was loaded with condiments.

Anne shook her head. "I'm not hungry. Not at all."

"Then why did you come?"

His directness made Anne turn away. She was uncomfortably aware of the shimmer in the air between herself and Robert Singleton. It had been there all along. The shimmer of attraction?

"I don't know," she murmured, shrugging lightly. More than ever her inner voice was telling her to leave. But she couldn't seem to make herself move.

"I'm glad you did. Jamie misses his mother."

Anne glanced at him suspiciously. "I'm not his mother."

"You're female. That helps."

"I'm back!" Jamie announced, his face alight with pleasure at having accomplished his task. He set the cans of soda on the table and rubbed his hands together to warm them. "They're cold!" he explained unnecessarily to Robert and Anne.

Robert laughed. "Of course they are. We wouldn't want to drink them warm, would we?"

"I like orange soda warm!"

"I give up!" Robert teased. Then he gave Jamie another task that also involved Anne. "Why don't you and Anne find a place for the quilt while I finish up here."

The child grabbed the folded quilt from the sand near their feet and hurried to grasp Anne's hand. He tugged her toward a spot he picked out. They had just spread the colorful square of material on the ground when Robert arrived carrying a set of plates loaded with hamburgers, potato chips and baked beans. He handed one to Jamie and Anne, and kept one for himself.

Anne gazed at him in silent protest, but he merely smiled. "Like I said, you look as if you could use a good meal ... and this is the best I can do at the moment. Eat what you want. We'll give the rest to the gulls."

Anne folded herself onto the quilt, the aroma coming from the plate making her stomach grumble in interest. She hadn't been eating particularly well lately.

She didn't mean to, but she ate her hamburger and the beans, although she gave Jamie her chips—which he happily accepted, interspersing his bites with happy chatter.

Finally, the boy was unable to sit still any longer, and he jumped to his feet to begin an exploration of the nearby rocks and sand.

"Stay in the cove," Robert called.

"I will!" Jamie promised as he happily stalked a seabird that ran along the edge of the water for a few seconds, before lifting into effortless flight. Jamie imitated the bird's flapping wings, and even though he remained firmly on the ground, he didn't seem bothered in the least.

The man chuckled fondly at the sight, and the sound rippled along Anne's nerve endings. To give herself something to do, she gathered the used plates and stacked them on the sand across from her.

"That was good," she said. "Thank you."

Robert shrugged. "Have another. I made extra."

"No, that was more than enough—more than I've eaten in one sitting in an age."

Robert stretched out lazily on his elbow. "Oh?" When after some seconds had passed she still made no explanation, he asked, "Have you been ill?"

"What makes you ask that?"

"You're pale . . . on edge."

"Possibly that's natural for me."

Robert shook his head. "No, I don't think so." He was quiet for a moment. "Then it must be something else. Something I'm an expert at: a broken love affair."

Anne made no denial. She got to her knees, preparing to take her leave. The conversation was becoming much too personal.

"Aren't you going to ask how I became an expert?" he prompted.

"I thought the answer was obvious."

He laughed. "You're sharp. I like that."

"I have to go. Thank you for the meal. I—"

His hand came out to stop her. "Surely you don't have to run off yet. Relax, stay a while. I haven't talked to an adult in almost a week."

Anne remained as she was, yet her body was stiffly held. She should go! Didn't she already have enough trouble without asking for more?

Her clear unwillingness to linger challenged Robert. Normally he had little difficulty in persuading women to stay with him.

"Jamie's mother and I are divorced. What about you?"

"I'm single."

"Never been married?"

"No."

Relying on practiced skills, Robert let his fingers trail slowly along the sensitive smoothness of her skin. "I'm sure it's not because you haven't been asked."

Instinctively Anne pulled away.

"No, don't," he murmured, smiling softly.

Anne could scarcely believe what was happening. His touch was sparking a reaction in her that was stronger than any she had ever felt before. A great shudder passed through her body as his hand continued to move. When it dipped forward, coming dangerously close to the curve of her breast, she made a strangled sound and jerked away, struggling to her feet, struggling for composure.

Robert was surprised by the suddenness of her action, the determination behind it. He quickly got to his feet as well.

"I can't—" she began, flustered.

"Look, I—" He reached for her arm again.

More to herself than to him, she said vehemently, "No!"

Without either of them being aware of his arrival, Jamie ran up to them at that moment. He was panting from his dart across the sand. He looked from his father's tight features to Anne's pinched misery, and his uninhibited smile faded. "Is something wrong? Did you get hurt, Anne?" he asked with concern.

Anne couldn't answer him. His innocent question seemed to encompass so much. Had she been hurt?

Everything had hurt her recently: first the people of the town, now an encounter with a near-stranger on a beach.

Tears rushed into her eyes as she turned to run away.

"Anne, come back!" Jamie cried.

But Anne paid him no heed. Tears were streaming down her cheeks and all she wanted to do was reach the haven of her beach house.

Jamie stood very still at his father's side. He didn't understand what had happened.

Robert, his hand resting protectively on his son's narrow shoulder, felt the shiver that passed through the boy's thin frame. He wanted to drop to his knees, enclose him in his arms and tell him not to worry, that he was here to take care of him now, that he would never let anyone or anything harm him ever again. But he held back, afraid that he had not yet earned the right, afraid that he might not be allowed to keep his word. Instead, he gave Jamie's shoulder a gentle squeeze of reassurance.

"Why did she run away, Daddy?" the boy asked quietly. "Did I do something wrong?"

Robert shook his head. "No, you didn't do anything wrong."

But Jamie detected a quality behind his father's words and he knew something had happened.

Robert touched his son's sun-warmed hair. *Some kind of father you are,* he scolded himself. *Can't let anything go—always out to prove yourself, no matter who might get hurt.*

Robert closed his eyes, regretting the past few minutes, regretting the passage of years. Silently he swore that he would change his ways, be a better father, a better human being.

And one of the first places to start was his attitude toward women. For most of his life women had represented a game to him—easy conquest, easy leave-taking. Except for Karen. And he had only gotten caught then because of carelessness.

He looked at Jamie—the issue of that carelessness—who was an almost exact replica of himself at five. *Yeah, old pal,* he mused, *you've known for weeks that you were going to have to grow up sometime. It might as well be now. It* has *to be now.*

ANNE REMAINED INSIDE THE HOUSE the next day, curtains drawn, artificial light giving brightness to the rooms. She didn't want to go outside, to feel the pull of the sun. Her head ached from the tears she had shed, and her eyes felt puffy.

She didn't know what she was going to do. She had thought that she was getting better, that she was learning to take everything in her stride, almost to the point where she was contemplating going back to Overton one day—to show the people that she hadn't been crushed. Then last evening had happened.

She rubbed the back of her neck, trying to ease the ache in her head. All the way around, she had acted like a fool. In the first place, she shouldn't have gone. In the second place, how was she ever going to get her life back to a functioning state if her emotions remained so close to the surface? She should have been able to handle him, to handle herself. Her experience with men wasn't great, but she knew how to say no—how to get the message across without creating a scene. Her cheeks burned when she remembered her hasty retreat.

Anne rose from the couch, planning to go into the bathroom to find an aspirin, when a muffled knock sounded on the shuttered patio door. She became perfectly still.

"Anne?"

It was his voice. She didn't answer.

"Anne? Are you in there?" He waited several seconds. "Look, I'm sorry about what happened last night. I really didn't mean—" His words dried.

Anne still said nothing. She waited, almost without breathing, for him to leave.

His shoes scuffed the wooden deck. "I feel stupid talking to a door—Jamie doesn't understand. He thinks what happened is his fault. He cried himself to sleep last night and this morning he's been moping around. I can't seem to convince him. Only you can do that. I know I came on a little strong. I'm sorry. I promise it won't happen again. If you'd just—" He sighed and thumped the glass door. "You're probably not even in there, but if you are, think about what I've said. Don't hold my behavior against Jamie. It's not his fault."

Then he left, and Anne sucked in the breath that she desperately needed before slowly resettling on the couch.

Jamie was upset. He blamed himself. The parallel to her own experiences as a child struck her strongly. Even to this day there were times when she had to fight to keep from blaming herself for what had occurred—the legacy of a childhood spent blaming herself for things that were truly not her fault. And where in the privacy of her room, she had cried herself to sleep night after night. It had to be her fault, she had thought then. Why else would her father not show affection for her as she had seen her friends' fathers do for them? She loved him so much. Was she not pretty enough? Not smart enough? But no matter how hard she tried, he never seemed to notice. Growing up had shown her the fallacy of her reasoning—that the problem had been in her father and not in herself. But she never forgot how easy it was for children to take the failings of others onto themselves, especially the failings of the people they loved.

She would have to talk with Jamie, and try to explain. Only it would have to wait a bit. If he saw her in the state she was in at that moment, it would only upset him more.

Anne ran a hand through her tumbled hair, pushing it back from her face. It was odd how separate events could merge, twisting in and out, finding a similarity.

ANNE STEPPED ONTO the deck later that afternoon, ready to find the boy. She had showered and put on makeup, so that she now felt more human—when she heard a noise come from the pool below.

Instinctively she pulled away from the stairs, remembering—always remembering—the fear she had experienced in Overton. Castigating herself for her timidity, she looked over the railing. In the beginning she saw nothing. Then, as she looked more closely, she saw a submerged form move under the glittering reflection of the sun. The form was small and quick as a seal, gliding through the crystal-clear water of the pool as if born to it. A head popped through the surface of the water. It was Jamie.

Anne stared in momentary disbelief, both that he could swim so well for someone so young, and that he was here at all. His father had said he was upset, and she had spent hours remembering things about her own childhood that she would much rather forget. But this child didn't look upset. He was having a fine time: coming to the surface, taking in air, diving under again. She watched as he sailed smoothly along the bottom of the pool before once again surfacing.

Anne's lips clamped together. Robert Singleton had lied to her. It was as simple as that. For what purpose, she had no idea. But proof that he had done so was at that moment splashing about in her pool.

Anne started down the stairs.

Jamie's head broke the surface of the water just as she took the final step onto the cemented patio. His pale hair was plastered against his head. When he saw her, he paddled in her direction.

"Would you like to tell me what you're doing here?" she demanded as she, too, closed the distance between them.

Jamie's usual urchin-like grin wasn't present in the solemn little face that looked back at her. He hooked his elbows over the edge of the pool and asked, "Are you still mad at me? I told you I was sorry." He uncurled a fist and a small stone dropped to join the collection of others on the cement. "I was gettin' the rocks."

Anne stared at the tiny mound and a second later her gaze switched back to the child. "You've been diving for rocks?" she echoed.

Jamie nodded.

"All this time?" she asked.

"I think I got most of 'em. They're the same color as the bottom, so it's hard to see."

Anne felt her displeasure melt. She had jumped to the wrong conclusion, been too quick to react. Conscience-stricken, she motioned for the boy to come out of the water. "You don't have to look for more."

"But I want to!" Jamie protested, staying where he was. "I promised."

"You've done enough. Look how many you've found."

Jamie dismissed the collection. "I want to look again," he said stubbornly, and without waiting for her consent, he slid away from the side and into the depths of the water.

Anne watched his smooth, economical movements. For such a young child, Jamie was very advanced—both in ability and in logic. Most five-year-olds thought more about themselves than other people. It was only natural that if they had thrown rocks into a pool, someone else would have to get them out. They certainly wouldn't retrieve them voluntarily.

Struck by that thought, when the boy resurfaced she asked, "Does your father know what you're doing?"

Since he had captured no rocks, Jamie was content to clamber over the side to sit with his feet dangling in the water. He shrugged, evading her gaze.

Anne changed directions. "Why do you think I'm angry with you?"

Again a light shrug, but this time he glanced at the pebbles. Finally, he said miserably, "You weren't very happy when you left yesterday."

Anne hunched down beside him. "But that wasn't because of you! It wasn't your fault!"

"You were mad at my dad," he stated, as if the thought didn't surprise him. He began to play with a stone, knocking it around but not really enjoying the game. "My mom gets mad at him sometimes, too. They argue about me."

Anne didn't know what to say, but as she continued to gaze at his face, at the much too early striving for adult control that was necessary to cover the hurt beneath, she said gently, "That's not your fault either."

His blue eyes turned on her. "Sometimes it is. When I'm bad."

"All little boys are allowed to be bad at times."

"That's what Daddy says." Jamie looked away.

Anne took a silent breath. *Don't get too deeply involved,* caution warned. But when she saw the vulnerability in the child's face . . .

Jamie's head jerked around, his attention drawn to the over-grown area outside the low fence.

Anne followed the direction of his gaze and saw Robert Singleton standing there, very still. He was watching them, listening to what they were saying. No emotion—either humor or concern—showed in his expression.

"I gotta go," Jamie mumbled, hopping to his feet and running the distance to his father. He stopped a few inches from the fence.

Father and son looked at each other, and after a few seconds Robert said quietly, "Go to the cottage and wait for me."

Even from the distance Anne could see Jamie swallow. Then he was over the fence and making his way down the embankment.

She started to call to him but was prevented from doing so by his father's steady gaze. Involuntarily Anne followed Jamie's motion of swallowing, but her motive was not the same. Her nerves had tightened immediately upon seeing the man. Last night and the time before had not been anomalies.

As he stepped over the fence and walked toward her, Anne rose to her feet.

He stopped a few paces away. "I'm sorry Jamie bothered you," he said evenly.

"He didn't bother me," she denied.

"He was supposed to stay in the cove."

There was a brittleness in the air about them. He wasn't saying all that he wanted to say and neither was she. Finally she murmured, "I tried to explain that I wasn't angry with him."

"So you were there," he murmured, referring to his unacknowledged visit. "Did it do any good?"

"I don't think so."

The blue eyes brooded. "He's too sensitive."

"A person can never be too sensitive," she defended, thinking of the hardness of her father.

"For his own good," Robert countered, changing what she had thought to be a complaint into parental concern.

"He's a very nice little boy," she said quietly.

"You can thank his mother for that."

"And not you?" For something to do, she moved toward the wisteria-covered sun shelter. When she

darted a quick glance at him, she saw that he was following.

"Up until a few months ago I hadn't seen the boy
in almost five years."

Anne sat down, using the motion to cover her surprise. There was such a strong bond between father
and son. She was amazed that it had been built so
quickly.

"You were away?" she ventured.

Robert nodded, looking out over the Pacific. "In
Southern Asia—India mostly. I work as a foreign
correspondent for a wire service."

A newsman. That fitted. He was of the same breed
that had added to the misery of her life, both during
and after the trial.

"You don't look as if you approve," he said, making her aware that his gaze had shifted back to her.

"It's none of my business to approve or disap-
prove. I'm a stranger to you."

"Jamie's taken quite a liking to you."

Let the man deal with his own problems! "So what
do you want me to do about it?" she asked, trying to
sound flippant.

Robert Singleton hesitated and for the first time
Anne realized that he wasn't as cocksure about everything as she had thought. And somehow that idea reassured her because it gave proof that she wasn't the
only person caught up in something that at times
seemed so overwhelming as to be insoluble.

"I know this is a lot to ask," he said at last, "but
don't cut him out of your life. At least, not while
you're here. He needs a woman's presence right now."

"Maybe you should take him back to his mother."

"No!" The answer was sharp, determined. He sighed when he saw her slight recoil. "It's complicated, okay? I can't explain it all now. Just... I'm just asking that you see him once in a while. Talk to him. Let him talk to you. I'll—I'll try to make myself scarce when you two are together."

Anne fingered a delicate leaf. Once, not long ago, she would have happily volunteered her time. She liked children. But that was before her experience in Overton. Before she learned the value of withdrawal.

Then she thought of the boy and of her special understanding of how he saw the world, and she heard herself say slowly, "All right. I'll see him."

Five little words... words that couldn't easily be taken back. Empires had fallen with less.

Chapter Three

Laughter echoed into the clear blue sky as Jamie and Anne frolicked in the pool. For a week, the young boy had been coming over each afternoon, with his father delivering him and then picking him up an hour or so later.

To his son, Robert Singleton used the excuse that he had some paperwork to catch up on; Anne knew the real reason was to keep his word about staying out of the way when the two of them were together.

His present behavior toward her was wholly circumspect. It was as if his approach that evening on the beach had never occurred, as if the shimmering awareness had never been. They acted as polite strangers, except for the bond of his son.

Jamie jumped for the colorful beach ball she had thrown, caught it, and fired it back. His quick return took Anne by surprise, and the ball slid through her tardily upraised hands to bounce away on the cement.

Anne was laughing as she pushed through the water to the side of the pool, ready to jump out to the rescue. It was then she saw that Jamie's father had made a silent approach. He was holding the ball, a slight smile on his lips as he looked at her.

"Here," he said, tossing the light plastic sphere. Anne caught it with little effort.

"Daddy!" Jamie squealed, and swam quickly to the side. "Why don't you come play with us? There's room."

"I came to bring you back to the cottage."

"But I don't want to go! Anne and I are having fun!"

Robert Singleton's glance slid to Anne and then back to his son. "Anne might have other things to do."

"Do you, Anne? Do you?" Jamie turned pleading eyes to her.

"Well—" she hedged. During the past week she had come to feel quite close to the boy, and she suspected that the feeling was mutual.

"No, Jamie," Robert interrupted. "Even if Anne doesn't, I do."

"But—"

"You don't want to wear out your welcome, do you, sport?"

Jamie bit his bottom lip. He shook his head.

"Then come on."

Jamie looked as if he was about to give another protest but thought better of it.

He seemed so disappointed that Anne felt her conscience tug. She cleared her throat. "Ah—if you like... If you're not too busy later..." She had the attention of both father and son. Jamie was looking at her with big, hopeful eyes, his father with no expression at all. "I'm not the greatest cook in the world, but I can make a mean hot dog. Do you like hot dogs, Jamie?''

"Do I like hot dogs?" His inflection was his answer, along with a spiraling backward leap that caused water to splash onto both Robert and Anne. When the boy resurfaced, his face split into a huge grin. "Can we come, Daddy? Please—can we come?"

Robert wiped the water from his face and smoothed the droplets that had splashed onto his shirt. "I suppose we can," he answered slowly. His unusual eyes settled on Anne. *Are you sure?* he seemed to be asking.

She lifted her chin. *No, she wasn't sure!* But she had asked, and she wasn't going to revoke the invitation.

"It's nothing formal," she shrugged.

"Then we'll be here. What time?"

"What time is it now?" she asked.

Robert checked his watch. "Four-thirty."

"Come about seven."

"All right!" Jamie squeaked and impulsively jumped to give Anne a quick wet hug.

Anne stayed in the pool as Jamie's father wrapped a towel about the boy.

"See you later!" the child called as the two of them started carefully down the embankment.

Anne waved and then glided across the water on her back. A wide expanse of cloudless sky met her gaze. Had she done the wrong thing? Probably. But she liked Jamie. And this time, unlike the last, they would be on her territory. She would set the tone. Be in control.

ANNE WAS A BETTER COOK than she usually took credit for. To try to please her father, to have him take notice, she had often spent entire afternoons in the kitchen as she was growing up, testing this recipe, testing that one. That she never gained her desired reaction had not dimmed her hope that one day he would compliment her on her efforts.

She prepared a special potato salad along with a bowl of fruit ambrosia and put both in the refrigerator to chill. Then she checked on her supply of potato chips.

As she was coming out of the bathroom after a quick shower to wash the pool's chlorine from her skin and hair, she thought she heard a slight noise outside.

She automatically tensed, then smiled to herself. Something similar had happened twice before, and each time it had been Jamie. This time would prove no different. He had probably become impatient and decided to sneak over early. She checked her watch; it was nearly seven.

Anne hummed to herself as she dressed and dried her hair. The way the boy swam, she knew she didn't have to worry about him falling into the pool. Afterward she went to stand on the deck.

She had planned to use the patio table, on the lower level where the growth of wisteria would shade them from the bright rays of the setting sun.

As she tried to see if Jamie had already installed himself there—she didn't see him anywhere else—she leaned against the railing. And suddenly she felt herself tilt forward. The railing was giving way!

She uttered a little cry. She was going to fall!

Her free hand flailed, clawing at nothing but air. Then miraculously, it found purchase: a metal rod, running perpendicular to the deck was within her grasp.

She clung to the rod, her heart hammering in her throat, her body cold from fright. She had no idea of its purpose, but if the rod hadn't been there, she would surely, at that moment, be lying broken on the cement below.

Voices came from the embankment. Anne raised her head in time to see Jamie and his father come into sight. Jamie looked up to wave at her.

Anne swallowed. Her breathing still wasn't regular. She couldn't speak—couldn't move.

They crossed the fence and came to stand at the bottom of the stairs. She felt Robert Singleton's eyes run assessingly over her.

"Hi, Anne. We're back!" Jamie grinned.

Anne tried to smile in return but her effort was poor.

"Is something wrong?" Robert asked. A frown had settled on his brow.

"I—" Anne swallowed then tried again. "I almost fell."

Robert's frown deepened. "Stay down here," he directed Jamie and climbed the stairs to Anne's side.

"You almost fell?" he questioned, unsure that he had heard her correctly.

She nodded, pointing to the railing. "Be careful!" she warned as he stepped closer to shake it. Much more pressure and it would no longer be standing.

"Was it like this before?" he questioned, turning to her.

"No, I—"

"Has something hit it?"

"I don't think so. I—I haven't leaned on it so hard before, but—"

"You need to be careful with these things. Never lean your weight against one."

"No," she agreed, remembering the stark terror she had felt. "I won't. Not ever again."

His expression relaxed and he examined the wood more closely. "Looks like some nails have come loose in a couple of spots. Do you have a hammer?"

"There're some tools in the garage. I—I'll go see if I can find one."

Robert Singleton nodded, continuing to examine the full length of the railing.

As Anne moved away, her knees were shaky, but by the time she returned she had regained most of her poise.

"It's not very big, but it's the only one I could find." She handed him the hammer.

He took it. "Just so long as it hits," he said and then cautioned Jamie to move farther back from where he had come to stand directly below the deck. The boy promptly moved.

A few minutes later, the nails were back in place and Robert straightened. "There." He shook the strengthened result of his handiwork. "That'll do for now. I'll look around the cottage workshop and see if I can find something to reinforce the nails. In the meantime, don't lean on it."

Anne nodded.

"You okay?" he asked, examining her closely again. Her color was more faded than he had ever seen it, and the intensity of her hazel eyes still held a heightened, bruised look.

"I'm fine. I just—it just frightened me."

He smiled slightly. "I wouldn't doubt it."

Shying away from the side railing, Anne went downstairs. Jamie ran up and reached for her hand. "I'm glad you didn't fall." He paused. "Are we gonna eat soon?"

Robert, who had followed Anne downstairs, chided, "Jamie!"

Jamie grinned. "I'm hungry."

"Let Anne sit down for a bit. Okay? I think you'll manage to live a little longer without food."

Jamie led Anne to one of the patio chairs near the table and solicitously saw her into it.

"Just for a few minutes," she promised, smiling at him. A butterfly caught Jamie's eye, and he ran off to chase it as it flitted from flower to flower around the carefully landscaped patio.

His father sank into a chair across from her. "This is a pretty place," he said, looking around.

"Yes."

"Do you know the owner?"

She shook her head.

"Neither do I. I found the cottage in a newspaper ad."

A silence fell between them. Anne moved uncomfortably. Finally, he said, "Thank you for letting Jamie come over. He's much more content now."

"I enjoy seeing him."

"Still—"

Anne pushed hastily to her feet. She had just remembered the noise she had heard earlier, the one she thought to be Jamie. Only it hadn't been Jamie. Then the railing... Her mind recoiled from making a connection. "I—I think I'll get things started now. There's no use waiting."

Robert watched her hurry away. He couldn't figure her out. It was as if she didn't want to let anyone close, except Jamie, which left only himself as the person she didn't want to know. Was it because of the way he had acted the week before—coming on too strong, too quickly? No, it was more than that. She had been jumpy from the first moment he met her. It was something else. Something his years of experience as a reporter had picked up on and would worry until he found a satisfactory answer.

His gaze moved to his son, who was sprawled on the cement in the shade of a tall flowering bush, playing with something that was crawling on the ground, herding it this way and that with a tiny stick.

But then maybe he would just let it rest... let her keep her secret, if that was what she wanted. It wasn't as if he didn't already have enough to worry about.

DINNER PROGRESSED to a successful conclusion, with Jamie professing to like her potato salad more than potato chips, which was high praise coming from him, but passing on the ambrosia in favor of vanilla ice cream.

Anne leaned back in her chair and gave a small sigh as she watched the child finish his last bite. Before the meal started, she had decided to put her unease about the near-accident at the back of her mind. She was probably being paranoid; weeks of being the recipient of hate could do that to a person. But it was something she was trying desperately to overcome, and to help herself toward that goal, she had concentrated on each following moment with unusual intensity.

Robert glanced at her, his expression slightly bemused. "That was very good."

"Thanks."

"I thought you said you weren't a good cook."

Anne shrugged.

"I think I'd like to see you really fired up. You could probably give Julia Child a run for her money."

"Who's Julia Child?" Jamie asked, curious.

"She's a chef," Anne answered. "Which is something I'm not. I just mess around."

"We open a lot of cans," Robert confessed.

"I do, too—sometimes."

Jamie looked from one to the other and then gave a huge yawn.

Robert laughed. "You missed your nap again today, sport."

"Don't like naps," Jamie replied, his standard reply any time his afternoon rest was mentioned.

Robert glanced at Anne. "I've heard that before somewhere."

"Don't like naps!" Jamie said again, more loudly. He seemed to enjoy saying the sentence. He was grinning in the midst of his small rebellion.

"Your mother's going to be after my scalp—but then that's nothing so unusual."

Anne shifted in her chair. With the mention of the boy's mother, an edge had slipped back into the conversation. She glanced at Jamie and saw that his uninhibited smile had dulled. A quick look at his father revealed quickly masked pain. Did he still love the woman? Was that part of the problem she sensed he was struggling with?

Robert shifted in his chair. Why had he said that? Normally he tried to keep the dissent between himself and Karen well away from Jamie's ears. She didn't seem to care, but he did. The boy had enough to deal with without witnessing his parents' bickering. More than enough.

Robert glanced at Anne and caught her looking at him, causing her to quickly turn away. His glance then fell to the curve of her neck and from there to the scooped neckline of her sundress, where the soft material rested delicately on the beginning swells of each breast.

Suddenly the memory of the velvety texture of her skin came alive for him and he again experienced the pull of attraction. But this time he kept his reaction firmly in hand. He had promised himself that he was going to correct the error of his ways as far as women were concerned... and the attendant selfishness. Jamie was what counted now. He had hurt him more than once with his unthinking action. He would not do it again.

He stood, and pushed his chair close to the table. "Come on, son. I'd better get you home. Thank Anne for the nice dinner."

"Thank you, Anne."

"You're very welcome, Jamie."

The child followed his father's example, and pushed his own chair close to the table. His face had the mature look to it again that tugged at Anne's heart.

"Can we help you with the clean-up?" Robert thought to ask.

Anne shook her head. "There's not that much. You go ahead." She tousled Jamie's head. "See you tomorrow?" she asked him.

He brightened a bit. "Yes, please."

She smiled at him. "Then it's a date," she said softly.

His father's pale eyes drew her own. He was staring at her...as if perplexed by the contradictions of her character.

She met his look and held it, not letting him see beyond the surface she was working so hard to form. He looked away only when Jamie tugged at his arm.

"Are we going, Daddy? You said we were going."

"We're going." He folded his son's small hand into his own.

Anne's heartbeat had accelerated as Robert Singleton looked at her. She was very aware of his long lean body and the magnetism he wore like an invisible cloak.

He murmured something she didn't quite hear and turned with the boy to leave.

Anne said nothing, too shaken by her unwished-for response to do more.

ANNE PACED the living-room floor. She didn't need complications in her life right then. She needed simple days, simple nights, simple answers. Robert Singleton was a stranger. She knew nothing about him, except that his son had crept into her consciousness at a time when she sorely needed unquestioning affection. Jamie was a child. She felt safe with a child. But not with his father.

She opened the sliding glass door and stepped onto the deck. The ocean sounds were magnified in the night, the moon's silvery light casting an eerie loneliness on everything it touched. She started to go to the railing but, remembering, altered her steps instead. *Had* the sound she thought she heard been her imagination? And if it was not, what was it?

She shook her head, trying to free herself of all thought. Too many questions were whirling around in her brain from too many sources for her to come to any conclusions. She moved downstairs and across the patio to the embankment. Once there, she carefully picked her way to the beach below. Her body was restless. She needed to move.

A few moments later, she might have been the only person on earth. Only her footsteps showed in the sand in the moonlight; she was the sole benefactor of the chill ocean breeze. She rubbed her hands over her arms, enjoying the tingling cold, enjoying the elemental feel of solitude. She stood, facing the wind and water, letting her body be magically transported.

Sometime later—a half hour, an hour, she didn't know how long—she turned to make her way back to the beach house, her spirit soothed, her mind at rest. Now she could sleep.

But as she neared the embankment, she discovered that she wasn't as remote from the rest of the world as she had thought. Someone else was on the beach, walking with his head down and his hands stuffed in the pockets of his white jeans, his mind obviously troubled by something within him.

Anne slipped behind an outcropping of rock, thinking to hide, wanting to let him pass. He had not seen her.

But he didn't continue walking. Instead, he turned and stood, just as she had, looking blindly out to sea.

Anne remained where she was, barely breathing, gazing at Robert Singleton's straight back.

Eventually he bent for a small piece of driftwood and hurled it as far as he could into the dark waves. Then again, he stood, as still as a statue.

Anne's limbs were becoming cramped from cold. She shifted slightly, trying to ease them back to life, and the footing beneath one shoe crumbled.

Robert Singleton's head cocked and he glanced around in time to catch her attempting to steady herself.

"Who's there?" he called, his body instantly tensing.

Anne silently cursed her muscles' need to move. If she had waited just a few seconds more, he might have gone, and she could have returned to her house without him ever having been aware that she was present.

"It's . . . Anne," she answered, unwillingly revealing more of herself.

Some of the tension seeped from his body. "What are you doing here?" he demanded.

She continued to move forward until she was several paces away from him. "The same thing as you, I suppose. I couldn't sleep."

He hunched his shoulders and thrust his hands back into his pockets even as he turned to face the sea. "I wasn't expecting anyone else to be here."

"Neither was I."

He glanced at her and she saw a slight smile be born on his lips. "We crashed each other's party?"

"Not very much of a party."

"No."

He seemed disinclined to say anything more, as did she. But after several long seconds passed, he asked, "Would you like me to leave?"

She shrugged. "I was just going in."

She had started to move away when he said quietly, "Do you have to?"

She paused. "I think I should."

"Why?"

She was surprised by his question. "Because I'm cold and I'm tired."

"Is that all?"

"What more could there be?"

"You tell me."

"Good night, Mr. Singleton." She started to walk away.

She sensed his approach before she felt his hand reach out to touch her arm. When she stiffened, he immediately released his hold. It was too close a reminder of the immediate past.

"Do you think maybe we could just stay here and talk?" he proposed.

"What about?"

"I don't know." He ran a hand through his hair, disturbing its golden order. "Something...anything...the price of bananas! It just seems silly that we're neighbors and we can't exchange a civil word."

"I thought we had."

"Only when Jamie's around. If it weren't for him, would you talk to me?"

"Probably not."

"See what I mean?"

"But then I don't really want to talk to anyone."

"Why not?"

When she merely continued to look at him, he quickly continued, "I know I acted like a jerk the other day—and I've apologized for that. But it's something more, isn't it? And it has nothing to do with me. It's something you're running away from." His eyes narrowed. "Something about your face is familiar—"

Anne chose ridicule over retreat, hoping for a diversion. "Next you're going to tell me I look like an old girlfriend!"

He smiled. "Maybe you do."

"I don't find that particularly complimentary."

He shrugged. "Maybe it wasn't meant to be."

Anne frowned. "Have you ever tried to talk in English?"

"I write in English, remember. Most times that's good enough."

"Then write me a letter and possibly then I'll understand."

"I doubt it. Most times I don't understand myself."

Anne threw him an irritated look.

He laughed when he met her gaze. "We're talking," he prodded teasingly.

"Correction, we *were* talking." She turned away again.

"I'll remember, you know," he called after her. "I'll remember where I've seen you before."

This time Anne continued to walk, not even bothering to acknowledge that she had heard him. But she had. And his words echoed in her thoughts throughout the remainder of her restless night.

AT A DESERTED SERVICE STATION in the town nearest the beach house where Anne was lying sleepless in her bed, a man was hunched in a telephone booth, sneezing loudly from the cold he recently had caught. With the receiver to his ear, he waited for his call to be answered. Another racking sneeze shook his bull-like frame and he blew his nose into his already dampened handkerchief.

Finally, a gruff voice sounded along the long-distance line. "Yes . . . what is it?"

"It's me."

All traces of sleep quickly left the man who had been so rudely awakened. A squeaking mattress indicated that he sat up. "Did it work? Is it over?"

"Not quite."

"What do you mean, not quite."

"Just what I said. She ain't dead yet."

"Why not? What went wrong?"

"Just a glitch. It'll work all right next time."

Cursing came over the wire. Finally, "I'm paying you to do the job right. Don't bungle it!"

"It ain't been bungled."

"It better not be. It has to look like an accident."

"I'm good at accidents."

"That's what I was told . . . now *show* me!"

Another sneeze overtook the man in the telephone booth and he blew his nose noisily.

His misery was met with more cursing, then a loud click of disconnection.

As the man trudged back to his car, his heavy shoulders hunched even closer to his thick neck, the cold wind tried to pry between the collar of his shirt and his skin, and he shivered. He knew he had a fever.

What a hell of a way to make a living.

Chapter Four

Anne awakened the next morning feeling sluggish. She had gotten very little sleep the night before and wasn't particularly looking forward to the day, but Jamie was coming soon, so she hurried downstairs to clean the leaves and debris from the pool—something she did each morning before the boy arrived. Only, as she started to pick up the long-handled net, she noticed that the water wasn't circulating as it should. In fact, it wasn't circulating at all.

Her experience with swimming pools went only so far as one summer spent working as a lifeguard at a town pool when she was in her teens. But that was enough to tell her that the problem was in the filtering system.

Anne dropped the net and started for the pump room that was located at the far end of the patio. She hoped the problem was a simple one. Jamie loved to swim, and the pool was the only safe place for him to do so. The Pacific at this point on the coast was both too cold and too strong in current to be safe for a child.

Anne pulled the door open. The small metal room smelled damp and earthy from the array of garden tools and supplies stored along one wall. It was also dim; there were no windows. She stepped inside, leaving the door widely ajar.

Just as she had thought, there was no hum of electrical equipment to show that it was working. Her eyes ran over the filter pump and motor, searching for the location of the automatic timer. She would start with the simplest solution before working her way to complete incompetency.

She spotted the small metal box and stepped forward. It was then she noticed the puddles of water on the cement floor; the water was cold on her bare feet. She frowned. Had it seeped in when the sprinkler system sprayed the garden greenery? She couldn't see how that would be good for the things in the storage room if it happened each day...but that was one problem that wasn't hers to solve. She reached out to pull on the metal ring that would let her into the box.

The next second, lightning bit into her hand...shooting up her arm to her chest where a paralyzing jolt exploded, jerking her from her feet.

Even before she fell to the floor, she was unconscious.

JAMIE RAN AHEAD of his father, skipping in the sand, singing a cheerful song to himself, his thin body encased in a dark swimsuit, and a towel draped around his neck. He was happy; he was going to be with Anne.

Robert watched the boy with loving pride. His son. Sometimes he still found the miracle hard to believe.

Once he had thought he never wanted children—that they were more trouble than they were worth. And of course his father had provided him with many siblings. He'd had three wives? Four? With at least one child per wife.

To look at his father, no one would have thought him to be any great shakes as a lover. He was loud and boisterous and sometimes worked as many as three jobs trying to make ends meet because the children of each marriage always seemed to be left with him.

Robert, being the oldest, resented the life his father led and had vowed never to be caught in the same spiral. He had always used precautions in his involvements with women. Except once he had forgotten—

"Hurry up, Daddy. She's waiting!" Jamie stopped to call to his lagging father.

Robert's thoughts skipped to the present. He doubted that she would be waiting for him, not after the way they had parted last night.

Long after their encounter, he had stayed awake, trying to place the reason why she was vaguely familiar, but he had come up with nothing. Was it that she looked like someone he knew...or had known? Into his mind, though, had flashed a picture of her with a hunted expression: terrified, angry, afraid to strike out—but afraid not to. Where had the picture come from? Why was she running away?

Robert increased his pace to catch up with his son as the boy started to climb the embankment.

"Anne?" Jamie cried her name warmly, expectantly, as he topped the hill. "Anne, are you there?"

By the time Robert arrived at the low fence, Jamie had already scrabbled over it. He was at the base of the stairs preparing to climb them when Robert reminded him to be cautious of the railing.

Robert adjusted the wood bracing he was carrying. For the first half hour of this visit, Anne would just have to put up with his being there. If she wanted her deck properly secured, that was. For some reason the idea of making her put up with his presence appealed to him.

Jamie thumped loudly on the sliding glass door, then knocked again. "She's not here, Daddy," he said, turning puzzled blue eyes to his father.

Robert frowned lightly. She had invited Jamie back today. Surely last night's contretemps with him wouldn't have changed that. He glanced around the patio, wondering if his boast to eventually place her had caused her to leave for some place she thought would be more secure. If that was so, he cursed his tongue for what it had said.

He moved closer to the pool, examining the area once again, and his gaze fell on the small metal building with the open door. Something about the door bothered him.

Jamie was coming slowly down the stairs, his face clouded with disappointment.

Robert glanced at him and ordered, "Stay there."

The tone in his father's voice made Jamie immediately stop.

Robert approached the metal building with caution. "Anne?" he called, his body tensing as he drew near the door and looked inside. For a moment he saw nothing; then, on the floor, he saw her: crumpled, still.

Robert didn't waste further time. With quick movements he covered the distance between them and bent over her. He could see nothing around her that had caused her to fall. He reached for her wrist, automatically curling his fingers to feel for her pulse, while with his free hand, he smoothed the hair away from her face and pulled back each eyelid to check the response and size of her pupils.

She gave a soft groan and tried to pull away.

Robert transferred his hand to her chestnut hair, searching her scalp for a lump. He couldn't find one. There was a small abrasion but it didn't look serious enough to have been the cause of her unconsciousness.

Groggily she pushed at his hand, trying to make him stop touching her. "No—" she moaned.

"Anne! Anne, it's Robert. Can you hear me?"

His words made her struggle even harder.

Robert lifted her into his arms. Then he pushed to his feet, conscious that she was heavier than she looked. At the door, he twisted and ducked until he could point her feet through first and then follow with the rest of both of them.

Jamie's eyes widened when he saw his father carrying Anne from the room. He no longer stayed in place; he hurried over to reach for her hand.

"Is she dead, Daddy? Is she dead?" he asked, his eyes large.

"No, just unconscious," Robert answered as he walked toward the chaise longue beneath the wisteria blooms. Jamie was at his side. "Jamie—move the book to the table. I want to lay her down."

His son quickly complied.

Robert arranged her in as comfortable a position as he could manage.

By this time Anne had reached another level of consciousness. "Who...? What...?" she whispered.

"That's what we'd like to know." Robert took her pulse again. Where before it had been slow and steady, it now was racing.

When Anne jerked her wrist away and struggled to sit up, he gently pushed her down again. "Why don't you just lie there for a few minutes. There's nothing to rush for."

"But—"

"What happened, Anne?" Jamie crowded in. "Did you fall down and hit your head, too?"

Anne could remember nothing of what had happened. All she remembered was waking up that morning feeling out of sorts. Then, slowly, the pool and the failed pumping system settled in her mind, and she caught her breath.

Robert had squatted down at her side. She looked at him blankly. "I was reaching to check the automatic timer, and...and it shocked me! I remember reaching for it and then..."

"Then you're lucky to be alive. That floor was wet in there. In your bare feet you made a perfect ground."

Anne swallowed. Twice in as many days...her life had been threatened by something she had little control over. Twice in as many days!

"Are you always this accident-prone?" Robert asked, cutting into her thoughts.

"No. No, I—" A sudden chill went over her.

"I think maybe I'd better take a closer look at you. Will you let me?"

Anne's hazel eyes were huge with dawning fear.

"What is it?" he quickly responded. She had that look again, like an animal waiting to be caught.

No! Anne thought wildly. It couldn't be. It just couldn't be! The people of Overton had wanted to drive her out of town, not kill her! She was jumping to conclusions, letting fear push her past the point of reason. She had to make herself stop. The accidents had been accidents! Nothing more...purely coincidence. There was no ulterior motive. She had to get hold of herself.

She shook her head with unnecessary force, denying her thoughts, denying any possibilities. "No. I'm fine. I'm fine!"

A vivid picture jumped into Robert's mind. It was of Anne, surrounded by a mob of people... something about a trial.

"Daddy won't hurt you, Anne," Jamie said, trying to give her comfort.

Anne's body was trembling as she made herself sit up—a reaction to shock, a reaction to her thoughts.

Robert straightened. He took off the jean jacket he was wearing and emptied the pockets of the screws he was carrying. He wasn't exactly sure what he had done with the screwdriver and the bracing boards; he must have dropped them somewhere before going into the pump room. He certainly didn't have them now. He placed the jacket around Anne's shoulders.

The sudden warmth felt good to her. It was a measure of her distraction that she accepted the jacket unquestioningly.

"Sport, why don't you go upstairs and get Anne a drink of water. I think she could probably use one."

"Okay," Jamie replied, his expression one of concern. He was off and running almost before the word left his mouth.

"Don't run with the glass!" Robert called after him.

"'Kay," the boy returned, slowing down even before he had reason to.

Anne tried to straighten her hair, looking anywhere but at the man standing a short distance away from her.

"Would you like to tell me what you're afraid of?" he asked after a moment.

"I'm not afraid," she denied, not looking at him.

"I think you are," he contradicted softly.

Anne tried to stand but found that her legs weren't yet ready for her weight. She sank back to the chaise longue.

"I saw your face just now—do you think someone is trying to kill you?"

To hear the words spoken aloud disturbed Anne even more than her thoughts. "No!" she cried.

A moment passed. "I remember you now," he said quietly.

God! She had to get away! She couldn't sit here and...

"You were involved in a trial. Something about someone selling government secrets at a missile subcontractor operation..."

Anne covered her ears, a childish reaction.

"You were a witness for the prosecution. One of the main witnesses." As he spoke, his memory sharpened. At the time he had been involved in making arrangements for his and Jamie's month on the coast. Karen had been making life difficult, as usual, at first saying that the boy couldn't come and then saying that he could. Her husband had been behind her change of heart, Robert was sure, and he might have been grateful to him, if it weren't for the fact that the man was merely trying to push the boy out of his home. With Karen pregnant with his own child, Bryce Jennings made no secret of his prejudice against Jamie. But even in the midst of his own troubles, he had caught several newscasts about the trial Anne had been involved in.

He lifted one of Anne's hands away from her ear. "You can't hide from something like that—especially if someone is out to make you pay."

Anne jerked away. She got unsteadily to her feet. "No! I've told you that's not true. No one is out to get me."

"Then what's with the accidents?"

"Haven't you ever had an accident?" she demanded, finding refuge in anger. "Or are you so perfect that nothing would ever dare go wrong for you?"

Robert stiffened. "I think you know I'm not perfect."

"Then stop acting as if you are. Stop trying to tell me—"

"I'm just trying to get you to see what might be happening, and if it is something, to get you to acknowledge it and be careful."

"I am careful!"

"By standing barefoot in water while you work with something electrical?"

"I just touched the timer box!"

Robert was silent before saying, "I'd like to take a look at that box. Or is that something you'd rather not have me do, either?"

"Be my guest," she returned tightly.

"After I help you get upstairs."

"I can get there on my own, thank you."

"I think not."

He didn't give her time to protest. Instead of reaching out to assist her as she walked, he swooped to lift her into his arms.

"I'm not Jamie!" she protested heatedly.

"I'm well aware of that," he snapped in return, then with a face made of stone, he carried her upstairs and placed her on a couch before turning to walk stiffly away.

Jamie giggled after witnessing the proceedings. He handed her the glass of water that he had collected. "You looked funny with Daddy carrying you," he confided.

Anne gave him a tight smile and accepted the water.

ROBERT MOVED SLOWLY upstairs, his brow furrowed in thought. Nothing seemed to be wrong with the timer except that some of the inside wires were broken and were touching the metal casing, which made the box dangerous; then, when Anne had touched it... It could have been an accident. But when today's incident was put together with yesterday's, and especially considering Anne's immediate past, it would make a much less suspicious person than himself jump to a speculative conclusion. It looked as if the lady could be in trouble. Big trouble. Even if she wouldn't admit it. The question was, what could he do about it?

Anne was still sitting on the couch where he had left her. Jamie was at her side. When she looked up at him, inquiry and combativeness battled in her expression; she hadn't forgotten her unwilling transport up the stairs.

"So, did you discover anything?" she asked.

"Not really . . . a broken wire."

"Then it *was* an accident."

"I didn't say that."

"I refuse to believe it could be anything else."

Robert glanced at his son, who was following what was being said with interest. Anne copied the direction of his gaze. Jamie met her look and smiled tentatively, causing her to experience a rush of feeling for the boy.

She reached out to lightly squeeze his hand. "The pool might be a little cool . . . I don't know how long the heater's been off . . . but if you'd like to swim, it's all right with me."

"What about you?" Jamie asked. "Aren't you going to come in, too?"

Anne shook her head. "No—not this time. I think I'd just rather sit and watch you."

"I can show you my dives!"

"That sounds good."

Robert shifted position, causing her to glance around. "I brought something to fix the railing with and while I'm at it, I'll see what I can do about the timer."

"That's not necessary. I can call someone."

"I'm here. I might as well help."

Anne didn't see any way around it. With a stiff nod, she agreed.

SHE STEPPED OUT on the deck, after having changed from the one-piece swimsuit she wore when she swam with Jamie into shorts and a loose-fitting shirt. Jamie was splashing about in the pool, but his father was nowhere to be seen.

"Where's your dad?" she called as she started down the stairs.

"Over there," Jamie replied, pointing to the pump room.

Anne grimaced. She knew she shouldn't have hoped that he would change his mind. From the little she knew about him, he didn't seem the sort to back down.

She hesitated outside the open door, remembering the last time she had entered the room. Her fingers tightened on the jean jacket that she was carrying.

Robert looked up from his work and noticed her. "It's okay. The power's cut off. You can come in."

Anne was irritated with herself for acting tentative. She squared her shoulders and stepped inside. "Here. I thought you might need this."

Robert wiped his brow with the back of his hand. "Not in here." Inside the metal building the heat had risen along with the temperature of the day. "Put it on the table outside or something."

Anne nodded but didn't move. She was curious about the wires herself.

When he saw her peering at what he was doing, he leaned back so that her view would be better. "See . . . this was the cause of the problem. I'm wrapping it with some electrical tape I found over there." He motioned to the storage area. "It'll hold it for a while, until someone can replace it. The others look okay."

Anne understood very little about electricity, but she could see where part of the wire had come apart, exposing the copper-colored inside to the light.

"Where did you learn so much about wiring?"

"My dad was an electrician."

Anne handed the wire back to him. She started to turn away. Being in the building bothered her. Being in it with him bothered her even more.

"I don't think you appreciate just how lucky you are." He had gone back to work as he said the words.

Anne paused. "I've been shocked before, when I was a child . . . and survived."

"Electricity is funny stuff. You can never tell exactly what it's going to do. But the situation here was serious . . . especially with the water."

"Are you back to thinking that this was deliberate?"

"I think it should be given some consideration. How did the floor get wet?"

"From the sprinklers. They come on each morning to water the garden."

"This isn't the garden."

"The water seeped in. I don't know!"

"Or it could have been sprayed. Tell me, why are you here? Why aren't you in—what was the name of that little town?"

Anne reacted angrily. He had no business prying into her affairs! "The town's name was Overton...but I see no reason to tell you anything more."

"They didn't exactly like you for what you did, did they? I didn't see everything about the trial...I kind of came in on it at the end...but I remember a television reporter saying that the company the convicted men owned was destroyed by the scandal. The people couldn't have been happy about that. Small towns sometimes have a bad habit of revolving around one main source of income. Do you think one of the people could be angry enough to come after you?"

"I think you're a typical reporter," Anne replied quellingly. "Inventing stories if you can't find real ones."

"The press gave you a hard time, huh?"

Anne shut up. She had already said more than she had intended. She would not tell him more. She spun around to walk outside, her back stiff, her cheeks an angry pink.

That was the trouble with people from the media, she thought. They spent their days looking for trouble...until they got to the point where they saw trouble in everything. She sat down at the table beneath the wisteria vines. Jamie called to her to watch him dive. She waved agreement.

The little boy walked to the end of the diving board and executed a credible dive. She smiled and called encouragement when he surfaced. He immediately headed for the board again, flowering under her favor.

But even as she continued to watch him, she couldn't get Robert Singleton's suspicions from her mind—partially because she had entertained those same suspicions herself. Had someone followed her from Overton? Was someone angry enough to want to harm her? But why? She had already paid for her "crime." She had allowed them to drive her from the town. Wasn't that enough?

No, it couldn't be that. If it were, the person would have to be unbalanced. Which wasn't a bracing thought.

Anne reviewed all the people that she knew there—and having run the town's only print shop, she knew almost everyone. There was no one who would fit that mold. Overton had its share of slightly odd characters; every town did, but no one who was crazy enough to slip into the realm of murder.

She jumped when Robert came silently up behind her and reached for something sitting on the table.

He smiled wryly at her emotional giveaway. "Just wanted to get this," he explained, reaching for the screwdriver that she had been too self-involved to notice. "For the railing."

"You don't have to do this," she said stiffly.

"I want to."

"A jack-of-all-trades," she taunted.

"Jack's my middle name!"

Jamie had come to stand beside them, water pooling around his feet. "No, it isn't, Daddy. Your middle name is Allan, like mine."

Robert laughed and tousled his son's wet head. "I was just teasing Anne."

Jamie grinned. That was something he could understand. "What's your middle name, Anne?"

Anne could feel the beginning of a headache; it had been hanging in the background since she had awakened from her shock, only now it seemed to be growing. She rubbed her temple, unconscious of the telltale sign. "Elizabeth."

"That's a pretty name!" Jamie came to stand close beside her.

"It was my mother's." She smiled at him.

"Where's your mother now? Is she a long way away like mine?"

Anne placed her arm around the child's narrow shoulders, not minding the beading wetness. "She died a long time ago, honey. When I was younger than you."

Jamie bit his bottom lip.

Robert stepped forward to withdraw his son gently from her loose embrace. "Maybe it would be a good idea for you to lie down for a bit. Jamie and I can come back later to fix the railing."

She didn't want to seem quick to agree to any suggestion that he made, but if agreeing would ensure some time alone, she would do it. "That sounds like a good idea. Thank you, I'll do it."

"You're going to take a nap!" Jamie crowed.

"Just like you are," his father reminded.

"Don't—" Jamie began.

"—Like naps!" Robert finished with him.

Father and son laughed spontaneously, and Anne joined in with them, although not as enthusiastically. Her headache was increasing in intensity by the minute. She would be glad of a darkened room and some quiet.

"I'll switch on the pool equipment before we go," Robert told her.

While he was gone, Jamie reached over to hug Anne's neck. Then, surprising her, he planted a soft kiss on her cheek. "I love you," he whispered.

Anne wasn't accustomed to being the recipient of such uncomplicated affection. She reached up to touch his arm, her throat too tight to make a reply.

Robert ducked his way from the pump room in time to see his son standing close to Anne, giving her an embrace. He stopped. Then he came forward more slowly, giving them time to part.

When he arrived at their side, Jamie was flushed with pleasure and Anne couldn't hide the moisture that had collected in her eyes.

A HULKING FORM was seated in a car, staring into the distance. He had set everything up perfectly. And it had failed again. His employer would not be pleased. Unless he decided not to tell him...as in, what he didn't know wouldn't hurt *him*!

He tapped his fingers against the steering wheel. He would have to come up with something else—something that wouldn't miss.

He sniffed and wiped at his reddened nose. His entire body was achy and cried out for rest. He was having a hard time making himself think straight.

He remained still for several long moments, his tapping finger and an occasional sniff his only action.

The constraint he was under was difficult. If he could just walk in and take care of the matter, it would be infinitely easier. But he had to leave no trace. Raise no suspicion.

Slowly he began to smile, and the smile deepened as he thought his idea through.

He now knew of a foolproof way. He didn't know why he hadn't thought of it before.

ROBERT RESTED A FOOT on an outthrust rock, unconsciously staking a claim. His hands were buried in the pockets of his jeans and his head was lowered. He was looking at the rock, but his mind was far away.

Jamie was asleep. He fought his daily naps but Robert could see that they did him good. Still, he would have a talk with Karen when he brought the boy back.

When he brought the boy back... Robert made a pained sound deep in his throat.

What he wanted to do was take him away from the home where the child was made to feel a stranger, where he actively wasn't wanted by one of the principals living there. Karen loved the boy, he knew that. But she was so deeply under her new husband's influence that she was being torn in two. Then, to add to that complication, her pregnancy wasn't going well.

Robert remembered her first pregnancy—the one that had produced Jamie. That one hadn't gone well either. But at the time their marriage had been breaking up and he hadn't been sure if her mood swings were a result of the pregnancy or ill-feeling.

But to bring him back?

How could he bring him back when he knew Jamie was being hurt emotionally? It would be like asking him to tear off one of his limbs. He had deserted the boy once; he couldn't do it again.

Yet how could he take him away? Jamie loved his mother. He missed her. If he took him away, never to see her again, what effect would it have on the boy?

Robert didn't care about the trouble he would be in himself. He would happily face whatever punishment would be dealt out at a later time. What mattered was Jamie and his future happiness.

Only how did he go about achieving that?

Robert turned his face into the wind, hoping to find enlightenment from nature's silent song. But no enlightenment came, and his soul continued to carry its heavy weight as he slowly retraced his steps to the cottage.

Chapter Five

Anne awakened in the night, a cold sweat bathing her body. At first she was too afraid to move. She didn't know where she was, what she was doing, or why she was being threatened. She sat up in bed with a quick movement, her heart palpitating, her eyes trying to probe the darkness. All she could hear was the ragged intensity of her own breathing.

When she realized that she was in her own bed—or at least the bed she had been using for the past week and a half, and that there was no threat—not now, at least—she groaned and ran a hand through her hair, feeling the moisture that had collected there. Her gown was sticking to her skin; the sheets were damp.

Fear. She was reacting to fear.

But was the fear real? The shock had been real, the loosened railing . . .

She drew a deep breath and expelled it slowly, trying to gain control.

She had gone to bed almost immediately the previous afternoon, a raging headache driving her into the coolness of the darkened room, and she had fallen almost instantly asleep.

Now the headache was gone, and she felt that sleep might never come again.

She threw the sheet from across her legs and swung her feet to the floor. She had no idea what time it was; it could be anywhere from twelve to four. And the clock beside her bed was of little use. One of the first things she had discovered upon her arrival at the beach house was that the bedroom clock did not keep accurate time. But time hadn't mattered then. She had wanted to forget everything. So she had done nothing to alter the arrangement.

She moved into the bathroom and turned on the shower. When steam filled the room, she stepped into the cubicle, sighing as the heated droplets drummed against her head and shoulders, sliding blissfully down her back and over her breasts.

Was someone trying to kill her? The question wouldn't go away even though she felt ridiculous asking it. And if they were, what could she do? She could call the FBI—but would they believe her? She had no proof, only two mishaps. She couldn't go to them with so little basis in fact. And even if she could prove a threat, what would happen then? She was no longer a witness who needed protection. The case had ended. She was of no use any longer. They would probably tell her to go to the civil authorities. And the local police would be hard to convince.

Anne shook her head. She didn't have much choice. There was nothing she could do... except be wary. If she chose to believe that her life was threatened.

She stepped from the shower and reached for a towel, rubbing it over her body, over her hair.

How in the world had she come to this? Throughout her life she had been one of those people who quietly go about the business of living. She hadn't drawn attention to herself, hadn't tried to be something she wasn't. She had chosen to live in Overton after her move to the west simply because it was small. She could become lost, in a quiet way, in the life of the community; eventually she could fit in, become a part of it.

Then had come the day—that horrible day—when she had discovered the papers lying in the midst of the discarded copies. Accountants from Kinkaid Systems had descended upon her shop like locusts. Something had happened to the electrical system in the administrative section of the company, and they had to have copies of various reports to send to the government that afternoon. Her print shop was the logical place to get those copies, since she had the only facilities in town capable of handling such a large volume. She had worked along with the men and women who arrived there, putting aside other jobs that she had contracted to do, helping them in their frantic haste. Then they had left just as swiftly as they had arrived, in a flurry of anxious pressure.

The papers—she always thought of them as 'the papers'—had been among the discards. At first she had thought to call the company and tell them they had left something, then she had happened to scan the contents. And she couldn't believe what she was reading.

Anne padded out of the bathroom, a terry-cloth robe wrapped about her body.

She still didn't understand how the papers had come to be left in her shop or why they had been brought there in the first place. No one—no one who knew of their existence would have wanted them to be seen.

She moved down the hall to the linen closet and collected a fresh set of sheets.

If only she hadn't read them. If only she had seen the colorful letterhead and immediately called for someone to come get them.

Anne hugged the sheets as she returned to the bedroom. She had just put them on the chair, in preparation for removing the soiled ones, when a furtive scrabbling sound came from the deck.

Anne froze, her head cocked to one side, listening intently. The scrabbling came again, only this time it was accompanied by a crash. It could only be one of the ceramic pots that held flowering geraniums, falling to the patio below.

A scream leaped to Anne's lips. But she held it back. If someone was out there, she didn't want to alert him to the fact that she was awake. When an intruder came into a house at night, she knew the proper thing was to pretend to be asleep—for as long as it took the thief to leave. But she wasn't in bed—and the person who would come into her house might not be after her possessions... but her life! Remaining still would do no good.

Anne's thoughts immediately centered on escape. In her dreams, she had practiced such flight enough times. She should be an expert. But dreams have nothing to do with reality and she found that she had a hard time making herself move.

Another sound came from the deck, causing Anne's body to respond. Without stopping for shoes or for proper clothing, she ran to the front door and plastered herself against it. Her breathing was labored, her thought processes scattered. Yet she knew that she shouldn't just run outside. There might be someone there, just as there was someone on her deck.

Her hands unconsciously opened and closed as she tried to decide what to do.

Finally, she knew that she had to take the chance. She had to get out of the house. She couldn't just wait there for...

She jerked the door open and darted outside, not stopping to look back, not stopping for anything. She ran to the first cover that she could find: a juniper bush that grew alongside the driveway. She hunched down behind it, trying to catch her breath, knowing that she could stop for a few seconds only.

She peeped at the house. It looked quiet...but she could feel a presence. She shivered in the cold night air, her bare feet planted in the sandy soil.

What did she do now? Where could she go to find help? Her thoughts immediately centered on Robert and the cottage a short distance away. Without giving herself time for deliberation, she started to run, trying to blend into the shadows. She knew that her light-colored robe could give her away to whoever was at her house. Her only hope was that he wasn't looking.

ROBERT LAY IN BED, his arms folded beneath his head, giving height to his pillow. His mind was once again wrestling with his dilemma—what to do about Jamie; how best to handle the situation—when a loud knocking on the front door caused him to jackknife into a sitting position. The knocking sounded frantic, emphatic.

He jumped from his bed and slid into his jeans, snapping and zipping them on his way to the door. Once he arrived there, he didn't immediately open it, using the caution that years of living in dubious locales had taught him.

"Who it is?" he challenged. "What do you want?"

"It's me! Anne!" came the reply. Her voice was tight, hoarse. "Let me in. I—"

The door opened in a flash.

His eyes widened in surprise as he saw that she was standing on his doorstep, disheveled, wearing only a robe, her eyes frantic with fear. He started to speak, but she practically threw herself inside.

Her hand came out to grasp his arm, her fingers surprisingly strong. "Someone's at my house. They're trying to get in."

His body stiffened. "Did you see them?"

"No. I—I just ran."

She was trembling. He closed the door to keep out the terror, and saw her to the couch in the front room. She sank onto it, reflexively, almost as if she didn't quite know what she was doing. He sat down beside her, allowing her to keep possession of his arm.

"Tell me what happened," he directed.

"I—I was awake, and someone was on the deck. I heard them."

"Did they try to get into the house?"

"I don't know. I didn't"—she swallowed—"I didn't wait around to find out."

He smiled slightly. "A wise idea. Do you know how many there were?"

She shook her head, running a hand through her damp hair. She must have just gotten out of a shower, he thought, noting the lack of makeup; and, with another part of his brain, how pretty she looked without it.

"I don't know."

Robert thought for a moment. He didn't have the gun he usually kept with him on his assignments overseas. He hadn't brought it, purposely, because of Jamie.

"Would you like me to see what I can find out?" he asked, knowing that he could handle himself in most situations but not particularly comfortable with the idea of confronting a possible murderer without a weapon.

"No! No—I . . ."

At that moment, Jamie stepped into the doorway. He was wearing a pajama suit that was all one piece from covered feet to his neck. He was rubbing his eyes against the light his father had switched on, when he realized their nocturnal visitor was Anne.

"Daddy . . . What's happenin', Daddy? Somethin' woke me up."

Robert gathered his son close to his side. He thought quickly. "Anne's come over for a visit. Isn't that nice? And she—ah—she might spend the rest of the night with us."

Jamie focused on Anne. "She can sleep with me," he offered. "I wouldn't mind."

"No, I think we're going to talk for a while yet, sport. Why don't you go back to bed. She'll be here in the morning when you wake up."

Anne wanted to protest. Yet where else could she stay?

Robert released the little boy who wandered sleepily over to Anne to hug her before turning to take his father's hand. "See me back to bed, Daddy? Please?"

Robert glanced at Anne. Stay here, his expression said. She bit her lip and looked down at her trembling hands.

Robert was gone for only a short time. When he came back, he proposed, "Maybe we should call the police."

"What time is it?"

Robert glanced at his watch. "A little after three."

She chewed her bottom lip. "Do you think whoever it is will still be there in the time it takes the police to come all this way?"

Robert shook his head. He had no idea.

She sighed, hugging her arms across her breast. "I don't know what to do," she moaned. "I wish . . . I wish none of this had ever happened!"

Robert was silent. Nothing he said could change anything.

Eventually, when some moments had passed, he stepped close to lightly touch her arm.

"Why don't you try to get some rest. You can take my bed. I'll take the couch."

"I don't want to take your bed. It's already bad enough that I've disturbed you." She became aware that he was wearing only his jeans. She looked away from his nakedness.

"That's what neighbors are for. I told you that the first day we met."

"I remember," she responded. She also remembered her definite conclusion that she would never call on him. Never say never, an axiom to live by. She felt a nervous laugh well up in her throat, trying to push its way to release. She put a hand to her mouth to still it. He wouldn't understand. And she didn't feel up to an explanation.

IN THE END, ANNE spent the remainder of the night on the couch. Not that she got any rest. She merely lay in the darkness, waiting for the light of day, trying not to let herself think of anything that would cause her to panic . . . and being wholly unsuccessful.

Even under the blanket Robert had found to cover her with, she was chilled. Her very soul was chilled. She wished that she could go to sleep, and that when she woke up none of this would be happening. But she knew that sleep wouldn't solve this problem. This was even worse than what she had suffered as a child, or what she had suffered in Overton. Not being wanted . . . that was one thing. Being the object of elimination was another.

ANNE WAS SITTING on the couch when Robert entered the room early the next morning. The sun hadn't been up long. She wondered if he had slept after her arrival. He was buttoning the last buttons of his shirt as he glanced across at her.

"Good morning," he said, without a smile.

She murmured a greeting in return.

"I'm going to go over to your house and look around," he said without preamble.

She started to rise. "I'll go with you."

He shook his head. "It would be better if you'd stay here."

"But I want to go. It's not fair that I put this problem all on you."

"I've been in worse situations. I want you to stay here with Jamie."

She had temporarily forgotten the child.

"I don't want him left alone," Robert continued.

"Then I should go. I'm sorry I was such an idiot last night. It was probably nothing...just my imagination."

Robert didn't bother to reply to that fabrication. He merely smiled and stepped to the door. "I'll be back in half an hour. If I'm longer...here are the keys to my car. It's parked at the side of the house. Take Jamie and go to the nearest police station."

Anne caught the keys he tossed. She gazed at them as if they were alien beings. When she looked up, he was gone.

THE ROOM WAS TOO SHORT, too narrow. She felt closed in. And she didn't want to make any noise. She didn't want to awaken Jamie. She looked at the clock on a stone mantel. Twenty minutes had passed. Twenty-one. She resumed her quiet pacing.

She still didn't want to believe everything that had happened. It was too bizarre. She had never wanted to hurt anyone. But once she had read the papers left in her shop, she couldn't just forget what they said. When she first called the nearest office of the FBI, she had almost hung up once someone answered. Then she had found her voice, and stumbled her way through an explanation.

Why did the papers have to be there? Who had left them? The questions still circled in her mind. But most importantly, who was in so maddened a state that they were willing to take her life? It didn't make sense. The damage already had been done—to everyone, all around. So why follow her and do this?

The back door opened and Anne tensed. She waited with bated breath for whoever would appear.

Robert's vivid gaze swept over her as he entered the room. He saw the slight easing of her tension when she recognized him, an acknowledgement of the pressure she had been experiencing.

"Someone was there, all right," he said, without preamble. "One of the flowerpots had been knocked off the deck."

"I know. I heard it fall."

"And the table by your chaise longue was tipped over."

Anne nodded.

"But that's all I could see. No one's there now. I checked the whole place. I couldn't see that anything had been bothered inside."

"How did you get in?"

He smiled slightly. "I believe you left in a bit of a hurry. The front door was open."

Anne moved nervously. "Then I suppose there's no reason for me not to go back."

"I wouldn't. What makes you think they won't come back?"

Anne reacted with anger, not at him but at the situation. "Then what am I supposed to do?" She looked down at her form of dress, for the first time realizing how little she had on. "I can't stay dressed like this! I can't stay here!"

Robert shifted position, letting her anger roll off him. "Well, I thought about your clothes. And I took the liberty of bringing something back."

Anne stared at him. "You what?"

"I found some clothes and brought them to you."

It was just too much. Last night, in her extremity, she had come to him for help. But she could take only so much invasion of her privacy. "You had no right...!" she began indignantly, her anger now focusing on him.

He reached for the small bundle on the table behind him. "Don't get excited."

Anne swept it from his grasp, pulling it to her, stuffing the section of one of her lacy bras back into place after it had been dislodged by her action. Her cheeks were pink when she repeated, "You still had no right!"

His humor was increasing with her dishumor. "I didn't think you'd want to spend the next couple of days in your robe."

"I'm not going to spend a couple of days here."

"Think about it. What are you going to do tonight if the person comes back? Make another mad dash over here? You're welcome to, of course. But I should think that a little planning would save you the trouble."

"What are you talking about?"

"Just that while I'm over at your place you'll stay here with Jamie."

"But—"

"I don't think it would be a good idea for all of us to be over there. I don't want to put Jamie in any kind of danger. So it's only logical that I go over there while the two of you stay over here. Whoever it is won't be expecting me."

"But I can't let you do that. It's not your problem."

"Can you handle it alone?"

Anne sighed. "No."

"Then let me help."

"But you don't know me!"

"Jamie does. He likes you."

"Still . . . it might be dangerous."

He laughed lightly. "I'm not the heroic kind. I like my skin as much as the next person. I won't take any chances."

"What will we tell Jamie? I mean . . . if I'm here and you're . . ."

"We'll tell him the truth. At least part of it."

"You'll tell him before you leave?"

He nodded. "I thought I'd go over in a couple of hours and then stay put. We don't want to give away the fact that we've changed places."

"No—"

He looked at her closely. "What's up?"

"It's just—"

"What?"

"Why are you doing this?"

"Because I like excitement? Remember what I do for a living."

"I don't think that's all of it."

He shrugged. "Maybe not. But then I don't like to look at motives too closely. Never have. It's one of my failings." He frowned and motioned down the hall. "The bathroom's down there. While you change I'll see about getting us some breakfast."

"I'm not hungry."

"You never are, if I remember correctly. But I'll still fix something. Maybe smelling it will do the trick like it did last time."

Anne looked at his handsome face. She still felt the pull of his attraction. She turned away, making no reply.

"How late does Jamie usually sleep?" she asked, sitting across a small wooden table from Robert. He had prepared a light meal of fresh fruit and toast, and Anne had already speared several cubes of cantaloupe and eaten them. At the moment she was lightly buttering a half of a piece of toast.

Robert checked his watch. "For about another hour."

An hour. Anne felt better in the shorts and shirt that he had picked out for her to wear, but it still bothered her that he had collected her clothing. Anne was very much a person who kept to herself... at least in the more intimate aspects of her life. She didn't like strangers to...

She glanced at him from beneath her lashes. Could he still be counted as a stranger? When he was willing to do so much to help her?

He caught her look and smiled, as if he knew what she was thinking.

"I've met your kind before," he said, easily, conversationally.

"My kind?" she questioned, immediately on guard. She didn't know all that much about him, but she did know enough that when he made a statement like that, it was time to be cautious. He had a quick mind—quicker than hers, she was afraid.

"Basically, you don't like to rely on people. At least, not more than you have to."

"Is that wrong?"

"No. I'm something like that myself. But mine comes from years of independence. Yours... I'm not exactly sure where yours comes from."

"I think I should leave."

"The cottage?"

"The Coast."

"Where would you go? Do you have somewhere else in mind?"

Anne lowered the toast to her plate, untasted. "No... just leave. I'd find someplace."

Robert's eyes narrowed as he asked quietly, "Do you think that would solve your problem?"

"You mean, you think whoever is trying to hurt me would just follow?"

"It stands to reason if they followed you here."

Anne looked away. "I don't understand any of this."

Several silent seconds passed. "Would you like to talk about it?" he asked.

Anne bit back an automatic denial. She did want to talk about it; yet she didn't. Verbalizing it—going through all the pain once again—would be difficult.

"Possibly I can help you to understand," he urged.

Slowly, her gaze returned to his. "Would you use what I tell you?"

"In what way? Do you mean as a reporter?"

She nodded.

He gave his head an emphatic shake. "I'm not that kind of a reporter. I don't go in for dirt. Anything you tell me will be kept between the two of us. Anyway, I'm on leave. If I weren't, I wouldn't be in the States."

She was silent for another moment, debating whether to trust him. The various reporters at the trial had not given her much cause to believe in their integrity. But as he said, he wasn't that type of reporter. He was a correspondent. His field was foreign affairs. And he had already done so much for her.

Slowly, she began to tell him what had happened— from the mysterious appearance of the incriminating papers to her forced exit from the town.

When she finished, he laughed shortly, not humorously, and shook his head. "That's quite a lot to go through. No wonder you're a bit . . . sensitive."

Telling him had been an agony for Anne, especially reliving the antagonism of the townspeople. It hadn't been pretty to experience; but to admit to it, in words, was even more degrading. She folded her hands together to keep them from shaking.

"And you don't know who left the papers?" he asked, sitting back in his chair.

"I've no idea."

"It had to be one of the accountants."

"There were five or six of them."

"Do you think whoever it was left them on purpose?"

"You mean for me to find?"

"Exactly."

"But why?"

"To get you to do their dirty work. You said they were copying files for a government report. Neither of the two men convicted—what were their names?"

"Paul and Michael Kinkaid."

"The Kinkaids . . . you know neither of them would have wanted to let the government know what was going on. When the government found out, look what happened to them. But how did the person who left the papers get hold of them? And why did whoever it was choose you to get the word out? Do you know any of the accountants well?"

Anne shrugged lightly. "Just—just as people in the town."

"Not as boyfriends, not as lovers?"

"No."

Robert sighed. "It probably isn't that person anyway. I don't see why he'd have any reason to fear you."

"Fear me?" Anne repeated incredulously.

"Why else do you think whoever it is, is trying to put you away? For revenge?"

"That had crossed my mind after the way the town—"

He dismissed her proposal with a motion of his hand. "I don't think one thing has to necessarily go with the other. For revenge, they forced you to leave. They succeeded. Why do anything more?"

"But—"

"Someone is afraid of you. Do you have any idea who it might be?"

Anne was overwhelmed by the idea. She had been so afraid. It was hard to switch her mind to the possibility that someone else was equally afraid of her...if not more afraid. "I—I don't—"

"Think of all the people in the town. Did anyone act particularly different?"

"They all acted different," she responded with bitterness.

"Didn't you have any friends?" he asked curiously. "How long did you live in Overton?"

"Two years. I moved there from Ohio."

"Felt the call of California?"

"You might say that," she conceded. She wasn't prepared to tell him about her father's long illness and her need to start a new life after all the time spent nursing him.

"Did your friends abandon you, too?"

"I found out I didn't have any friends."

He shook his head. "Scandal does strange things to people."

"Everyone blamed me because Kinkaid Systems lost the government contract."

"Unemployment does strange things to people, too. Or the threat of it. Didn't they see the Kinkaids as traitors? After all, they sold a military secret to foreign governments."

"I don't believe they particularly liked that part of it...but, you see, the governments they sold the information to were friendly to the United States. And they figured they would learn about the missile component anyway. The Kinkaids were just doing it a little ahead of time."

"For money."

"Overton looked upon that as good business initiative."

"Kinkaid Systems was the major employer?"

"For Overton and several small towns nearby."

"And the other towns? How did they react?"

"They hosed down their streets as I drove away."

She had been looking at the table, but when she felt the force of his eyes resting on her, she looked up. In his eyes she read compassion. She lifted her chin. She hadn't told him the story to gain sympathy.

"Don't feel sorry for me!" she said fiercely.

"Did I say I did?"

"I saw the way you looked."

"I wouldn't want to go through what you have."

"I still don't want you to feel sorry for me!"

"All right. I won't!"

Anne stood up. She walked to the window that overlooked the ocean and hugged her arms across her chest.

He pushed away from the table as well. After he stood up, he said, "Well, that still doesn't tell us who's trying to kill you."

"I can't believe that someone is."

"Maybe they are, maybe they aren't. But can you take a chance and not believe it?"

Anne bowed her head. What was she going to do? How did she go on living? As he had said, if whoever it was had followed her here, what would keep the person from following her wherever she went in order to accomplish the task?

Right now, at this moment, she wished she were a child again...even with her father's stern coldness. At least then she wouldn't be threatened. Her pain would be entirely emotional. One day would follow the last in aching repetition. But at least there was a next day.

Robert had come up behind her. He took in the bowed head, the weary, frightened expression. He reached out to touch her, putting his hands on her shoulders—not in a sexual way, which was his usual want when touching a woman, but in friendship and in caring. It was funny, but he found that he genuinely cared about what was happening to her.

She turned her head. Moisture was swimming in her eyes with the threat of much more to come. She made an inarticulate sound, and he drew her back against him. He held her for several moments before she pulled away.

"Try not to worry," he said, hearing the sounds of his son's awakening. Soon he would be in the room and this odd little moment between the two of them would be shattered with Jamie's boyish enthusiasm. "We'll get to the bottom of this. I promise."

Anne held herself stiffly. It had felt good to be held against him... to feel his warmth, his caring.

It had felt *too* good.

Chapter Six

The tall, well-built man grimaced as he heard the approach of his assistant. He knew the man would want to talk with him about the latest downturn in the town's economy. When Kinkaid Systems went, it had a ripple effect on the rest of the community. Everyone was having a hard time, running up debts, afraid to make a wrong move. Overton was coming down around their ears. Something would have to be done and done quickly—only that wasn't his all-consuming problem. His dilemma centered approximately one hundred and fifty miles to the west. In a beach house. Where a man, if he was as good as he claimed, was supposed to have taken care of the situation. Only he hadn't heard from him for the past two days. And that fact was driving him quietly crazy!

He had to pretend; he had to keep his cool. He couldn't let on that anything was out of the ordinary—if one could call these days in Overton ordinary. If it happened, correction, *when* it happened, he had to be above reproach. He had to be as shocked as everyone else when they learned of Anne Reynolds's death. He had to pretend to just the right amount of

dismay, mingled with shame at the way they had
treated her.

*It was terrible about the accident. Who would have
thought...? Maybe we shouldn't have been so hard
on her.* He could hear the old biddies now. Especially
those who had been particularly savage.

His conscience tugged, but he ignored it. Expedience. She had to be sacrificed for a greater good. His
good.

He braced himself and called to his assistant to
come in.

When was the phone going to ring with the news?

THE DAY SEEMED HORRIBLY LONG to Anne, even in
Jamie's energetic company. He easily had accepted his
father's excuse that he was going to be away for the
day, and possibly the night, and that Anne was going
to stay with him. To the boy, the day was a treat.

They played games, went out on the beach for a
short time—Anne always taking care that they stayed
in the protected area of the cove—and watched his favorite television program.

From time to time, in her partially distracted state,
Anne wondered what was happening at the beach
house. She wished that she had made Robert promise
to call occasionally to set her mind at ease. She also
forgot Jamie's nap. And, being the smart boy that he
was, he didn't remind her.

Because of that non-event, though, Jamie fell asleep
early in the night and when she carried him to his bed,
all he did was smile slightly in his sleep and snuggle
closer in her arms.

From that point, time seemed to pass even slower. She tried to watch television, but she wasn't an especially big fan of the medium and couldn't get interested in the comedy shows. In fact, she didn't think that even the world's best comedian could get her to relax enough to laugh.

She wished that she could remember the telephone number at the house, but she couldn't. And such a reminder of that first day when she had been so angry at Jamie's parents for not teaching the boy something so essential made her sigh with impatience at herself.

She wandered from room to room, carefully respecting the privacy of Robert's bedroom. Everything that she could see was neatly kept. Not perfect, but orderly.

She returned to the living room and switched the television set back on, hoping that its muted noise would keep her company. Then she flicked through a magazine, only to discard it without finishing.

Finally, her restless gaze centered on the photograph positioned on a nearby table. Jamie had told her that the woman was his mother. She got up to inspect it more closely.

The woman was beautiful, of course. She hadn't expected less. Big dark eyes, dark hair—how had Jamie managed to be born with his father's much lighter coloring? And she looked out on the world with confidence. Yet there was something in her eyes—sadness?

Anne put the picture back where she had found it, ashamed to be prying. Then she sank onto the couch and curled up against an armrest.

The night was going to be very long.

ROBERT SLIPPED BACK into the cottage shortly after the sun had brightened the sky.

He moved quietly through the den and into the living room, where he found Anne asleep on the couch. She was tucked against one end, her chestnut hair tumbled from sleep, her cheek resting against one up-drawn hand.

For a moment he merely stood there, studying her. Then he reached for the blanket that had been neatly folded on the opposite end of the couch and let it fall open to cover her. She moved under the sudden warmth but did not awaken.

As quietly as he could, Robert went to check on his son before moving into his room. The day and night had been long and he had not slept.

Within minutes, he joined the slumber of the other occupants of the house.

ANNE AWAKENED TO a soft touch on her cheek. Her eyes jolted open, immediately alert.

Jamie was smiling at her, his features so like his father's. Had Robert's smile been so impish when he was young?

Anne struggled to sit up, pushing her hair from her face, straightening her blouse even as she pushed off the blanket. She had no memory of finding it last night. But then she had no memory of going to sleep either.

"Daddy's home," Jamie confided. "He's sleeping."

"Oh." When had he . . . ?

"You think I should wake him up?" Jamie asked, interrupting her thoughts.

Anne swung her feet to the floor. Her muscles were tight, aching. She moved her shoulders and stretched her neck. "No," she said. "Let him rest. He probably didn't get in until morning."

"I wonder if he'll sleep all day. My other daddy sometimes does."

This was the first time Anne had ever heard Jamie refer to his other father. "He does?" she responded, wondering if she should encourage him.

Jamie nodded. "He works shifts. He works in an oil refinery. I have to be really quiet when he's asleep. Otherwise he gets mad."

"I doubt your father will sleep all day."

"No." Jamie frowned and then brightened. "You want to watch cartoons? Today's Saturday!"

Until that moment, Anne had no idea what day it was. "Tell you what, you help me make breakfast—do you want oatmeal again?—and then we'll watch the cartoons."

"Okay!" Jamie cried and immediately hushed himself. "I forgot," he whispered, grinning.

He followed Anne into the kitchen and climbed on a chair where he could reach the cabinet and the stove. "Daddy doesn't like me to do this, but I do it at home all the time. Mommy sometimes sleeps late, too. And I get hungry."

He reached into the cabinet for the uncooked oats and then leaned farther away for a pot. Anne measured the correct amount of water into the pot and handed it back to him. Jamie efficiently placed it on a burner and turned the mechanism on.

"She's gonna have a baby," he confided. "She sleeps a lot. Sometimes she doesn't feel good."

Anne nodded. She let him continue to talk.

"My other daddy, his name's Bryce, he tells me sometimes it's my fault. That I make her sick." He paused, a frown on his brow. "Can I make her sick, Anne? Mommy says everything will be fine after the baby's born. But I don't know. What if I make the baby sick, too?"

"You mean . . . like catch a cold?"

Jamie shrugged. He measured oats into the boiling water. "Daddy says I have to be careful with fire and with hot water."

"He's right."

"I try to be good. I try real hard."

"I'm sure you do." He was so earnest. His stepfather sounded like a horrible individual. Blaming the boy . . . making him feel guilty.

"Bryce doesn't like me," Jamie said matter-of-factly.

Anne reached out to hug the little boy. Even as her father lay dying, she knew that he didn't like or approve of her. Not even when she gave up a good job and came back to the house she had grown up in to nurse him through his illness. He had been a difficult patient, always demanding, always finding fault. But by that time, she had grown up enough not to let his barbed comments hurt her. They didn't have the power to damage so deeply. She had realized that he was a very unhappy man and was taking out his unhappiness on her, and that nothing she could do could change anything for him. But she could change things for herself, by not thinking badly of herself any longer.

"Why do you think he doesn't like you?" Anne asked, watching as Jamie stirred the cooking cereal.

"He says I'm noisy...that I'm a pest."

"How long have you lived with him?"

"Since I was two. I'm gonna be six next month. Daddy's birthday is this week. I don't remember how old he is."

The cereal was done and they moved to the table. Anne laid out two bowls and two spoons, and poured them both a glass of orange juice.

She sprinkled brown sugar on Jamie's oatmeal as he requested when he saw her using it on her own.

His mind seemed to have traveled from the subject of their earlier talk, but hers had not. It was easy to see that Jamie was having a hard time with his home life. Did his father know? Had Jamie opened up to him as he had to her? She wondered if she should broach the question to him...since he hadn't seemed hesitant in asking her questions about herself.

Which brought her mind back to yesterday and last night. What had he learned?

The morning, filled with cartoons, was almost more than Anne could bear. The loud noises, along with squeaky voices that all seemed the same, frazzled her nerves. To Jamie, though, they were high entertainment, and she stayed with the child, sensing his need to share his pleasure with someone.

Shortly before noon, Robert Singleton emerged from his bedroom. His eyes were tinged with red and a growth of dark blond stubble roughened his cheeks and chin. He was slipping on a fresh shirt as he came into the room.

Anne glanced around and then had to look away, her already disturbed emotional state receiving another jolt because of his attraction. She folded her hands in her lap, trying to still their tendency to tremble.

Robert came to sit in a chair opposite the couch Anne and Jamie were occupying. He winked at his son and smiled at her but waited until the cartoon finished before speaking.

"Good morning," he said at last.

Jamie jumped up and ran to his father to give him a hug. "You're gonna stay home today, aren't you, Daddy?"

"I'm staying home. Did you miss me?"

"A bunch! But I like having Anne here, too."

He ruffled his son's hair. "Did you keep her busy playing games?"

"She likes to play games," Jamie defended, almost too quickly.

Robert lifted his son's chin. "I'm sure she does," he said quietly. "Otherwise, she wouldn't play them."

Jamie brightened. He grinned at his father then slid to a position on the floor where he became absorbed in the next cartoon.

Robert glanced at Anne. "How about some coffee?"

She was instantly on her feet. She knew he didn't wish to speak of her difficulties in front of the boy. "Sure. Sounds great."

They moved into the kitchen.

"I really would like some coffee . . . do you mind?" he asked, pausing in his reach for the coffeepot she had left plugged in.

She shook her head, stuffing her hands into the pockets of her shorts.

"Want some?" he asked.

Again she shook her head.

He cut the dark liquid's strength with milk and then sat down at the table, stretching out one long leg and then the other. He sipped the strong brew and grimaced, but he made no complaint.

"I suppose you'd like to know what happened?"

"Of course."

"Nothing happened all day and most of the night. Then, around three...I heard something on the deck."

Anne's fingers tightened on the back of the chair behind which she had come to stand.

"I went to the door and waited. I'd already decided that I was going to flip on the light and jump outside at the same time, relying on the element of surprise. Only, when I did that, I was the one who was surprised." He paused. "I found the culprits...a pair of raccoons. They were nosing around the patio furniture and the plants. They froze when I turned the light on. Just sort of sat there and looked back at me...little hands curled and their eyes wide behind their black masks. Cute little things. They ran off when I clapped my hands."

Anne was long in replying. "You mean...it was raccoons all along?"

"They're probably what you heard the night before."

She slowly slid into the chair seat. "Raccoons!" Suddenly she wanted to laugh. All along she had been so terrified, when in actual fact she'd had nothing to fear at all. She did laugh. "When I think how frightened I was...and how I came tearing over here. You must think I'm an idiot!"

He drank more of his coffee. "If I thought that, I wouldn't have volunteered to stay at your house."

Her laughter eased. She wiped the moisture away from her eyes...relief had caused tears. "Raccoons!" she said, enjoying the thought.

"Raccoons didn't cause your electrical shock or loosen your railing," he reminded quietly, attempting to bring her back to reality.

But Anne's euphoria was so complete that she didn't want to credit the words of warning. "Surely you still don't think that was something sinister! I did, I know. But that was when I thought..."

"And you don't any more?"

She tilted her head, her eyes searching his face. He wasn't smiling. Her smile disappeared as she looked at him. "Do you?" she asked. She didn't want to believe it anymore. She wanted to be free. She wanted to start over, to make a new life.

His pale eyes examined her hopeful face. He didn't know. He truly didn't know. The incidents could have been accidents. He shrugged, not answering verbally.

Anne began to shift uncomfortably in her chair. She took a breath, ready to speak again, when Jamie rushed into the room and climbed onto her lap.

"Can we swim in your pool this afternoon, Anne?"

Anne adjusted the child to a more comfortable position. She glanced at Robert before answering both of them. "I don't see why not."

Jamie wiggled with happiness.

His father said nothing.

ANNE ENJOYED THE NEXT few days more than she had any since her arrival. She seemed to have found a new lease on life . . . a new enjoyment. She laughed more often and more easily. She got more fun out of common everyday things: preparing meals, washing and folding her clothes. She felt as if tomorrow was something to live for. And that she would live to see it.

She put the incidents out of her mind, just as she could now ignore the mean-spiritedness of the small town that had driven her away. Whenever she thought of Overton, though, she experienced a small setback to her new attitude, and so she tried not to think of it too frequently.

Jamie came over every day, as did his father. Robert never swam with them, though . . . contenting himself to watch. He never mentioned her earlier fear or his suspicion. Somehow, they had slipped into an easy camaraderie, a significant change from the first days of their acquaintance.

Laughing at Jamie's antics, Anne slipped into one of the patio chairs, dropping her towel onto the table. She shook her head lightly, using her fingers as a comb. She glanced over at Robert, who returned her look for several long seconds before mirroring her smile.

"If you'd like to come swimming with us, you may. I wouldn't mind," she offered.

"I may sometime."

Anne leaned back in the chair and gazed at the sky. It was a typical cloudless blue after the morning fog lifted.

"Daddy, watch this!" Jamie called. "Anne, you watch too!" he added.

The two adults did as he directed, watching as he completed a much more proficient dive than he had been able to perform before.

"That's great!" Robert called when the boy surfaced. Anne echoed his words. Jamie grinned and headed back to the diving board.

"Who taught him to swim so well?" Anne asked, finally voicing the question she had been curious about for some time.

"My ex. She won a lot of competitions in college."

Anne cocked her head. "No wonder."

Robert nodded. "Jamie has her talent."

Anne was silent a moment. Then, "I understand you have a birthday coming up soon."

His smile was slow. "How did you find that out?"

"Jamie. He wants to buy you a present."

"He doesn't need to do that. Just having him with me is present enough."

Anne recognized the depth of feeling in that answer. Instead of probing further, though, she said, "Not in his view. He wants to get you something special. So I was thinking...would you let me take him into town?"

"Which town?"

"The little one over the hills. I can't remember its name, but I drove through it getting here. It has a few shops. I think he'll be able to find something in one of them."

"When are you talking about?"

"Tomorrow afternoon."

"I can see the two of you already have this worked out."

Anne's smile broadened. "He's very persuasive."

Robert looked at his son who was swimming gracefully under water. Anne saw the love reflected on his face along with a haunting pain.

"He's a wonderful little boy, Robert. You can be very proud of him," she said softly.

His gaze switched to her. "I am."

"But—?" she murmured, unsure whether she should urge him on, yet feeling the need to. So much emotion seemed to be roiling beneath the calmness of his demeanor. She had seen flashes of it before, but had never pressed. Now, she felt, was the proper time. Also, she wanted to be sure that he was aware of Jamie's circumstances in his mother and stepfather's home.

"What makes you think there are any buts?"

He was closing up, not letting her near. "Because so often there is some kind of qualification."

"Are you speaking from experience?"

"Doesn't everyone?"

Robert's eyes were narrowed. He sat perfectly still. Then he patted his shirt pocket, searching for something that wasn't there, if she read his expression correctly. "God, I could use a cigarette."

"Are you trying to quit?"

He nodded.

"Because of Jamie?"

He nodded again.

"You'd do just about anything for him, wouldn't you?"

"He's my son."

Anne proceeded carefully. "Has Jamie ever talked to you about his life at home?"

She had his full attention. "What do you mean?"

"Is he happy there?"

"What makes you ask that?"

"Just something he said."

Robert stood up. He stuffed his hands into his jeans pockets. "What did he say?"

Anne hesitated. Possibly she shouldn't be doing this. After all, Jamie was his son, not hers. But she couldn't live with herself in the future, when Jamie and his father were no longer a part of her life, if she didn't try to do something to help the boy. "Just that his stepfather doesn't like him. Do you think that's true? Or is Jamie just making it up?"

Robert's features were taut. He rocked back on his heels before resuming his previous stance. "I don't think he's making it up."

"So he's told you."

"Yes."

"What are you going to do about it?"

Robert spun around, sudden anger in his coiled frame. She was touching on a sensitive nerve. "Just what the hell *can* I do about it? I deserted him. When he was born, I was thinking about my career. I left him with his mother. I can't come back now and complain about the job she's doing."

"But if he's unhappy there . . ."

"He loves his mother. I thought you knew that."

"I do!"

"Then you see my problem."

Anne looked away. As usual, there was no simple answer. She felt Robert settle back in the chair. His voice was low as he continued, "I hate like hell what's happening. But I don't see what I can do to change it."

"Could you talk with his stepfather? Maybe tell him..."

"It would only make the situation worse. Bryce Jennings hates my guts."

Anne was silent another moment. "Have you thought about asking for custody...or partial custody?"

"Karen wouldn't hear of it."

"Why? Because you might go back to...India, or wherever it is?"

He raked a hand through his hair, disturbing it. "I'm not sure what I'm going to do."

Anne had no other suggestions. In the circumstances, the prospects for Jamie's future didn't look promising. She glanced at Robert's stony countenance. Now she understood a little more about what was driving him, what was causing that look of nagging pain. But in this case, understanding was no help.

ROBERT LISTENED with half an ear while Jamie chattered. They were walking along the beach, returning to the cottage after spending the afternoon with Anne. He glanced at his son's bouncing head.

So much had changed in his life over the past few months. He had given up a job—temporarily, at least—found his son, and was now struggling with emotions he had never been brave enough to face before.

Was this what life was like when a person no longer chose to hide from it? He wasn't sure that he was strong enough to cope. He wanted happiness for his son. If he left him where he was, he would face nothing but mounting problems. But if he took him away—in one way or another—would that solve the problem or only create additional ones? Any direction he turned, he was stymied. And yet he couldn't just walk away. Jamie had come to depend upon him. He saw it. Anne saw it.

Robert unconsciously shook his head. He didn't understand exactly what he thought about her, what he felt. Protectiveness...yes, in an odd sort of way. She looked like she needed someone to take care of her almost as much as Jamie did. And yet there was something more. If he had put that conjecture to himself some years before, he would have slept with the woman and been done with it. That had been his usual solution to such a dilemma. But with Anne, after their initial contretemps, he had held back. Not that he wasn't attracted to her, because he was. It was just...he had made a promise to himself and he was trying to stick to it.

No, that wasn't the entire truth. It was something in her. A hurt that he sensed. A hurt that went deeper than the disapproval of the town that had turned against her. Yet he didn't know her well enough to question her further. He respected her privacy—a situation she might find hard to believe, considering his choice of career and the trouble she had experienced with people of his ilk. But he *did* respect her privacy.

Jamie continued to jump ahead of him as they neared the pathway to the cottage.

Respect...an old concept. One that wasn't honored enough in today's high-powered world. Respect took time to grow. It wasn't something instant with immediate gratification. It grew and built until finally—

His train of thought was cut off by Jamie tugging on his arm.

"Can we have waffles for dinner tonight, Daddy? Please, can we have waffles?"

Robert smiled fondly at his son. Tonight, they would have waffles. Tomorrow, they would double up on vegetables and proteins.

Chapter Seven

Jamie's hand was warm and slightly damp in Anne's hand as they walked along the sidewalk of the town that at one time must have been a thriving fishing village and was now barely alive.

Several small shops did desultory business, catching the occasional vacationer and serving the far-flung occupants of this part of the rugged northern coast. One of the shops was a general store of sorts, and Jamie pulled her in its door, drawn by the models of wooden sailing ships given prime position in its front window.

"You think he'd like one of those?" Anne asked.

"He likes ships," Jamie confided. "He told me he did."

The proprietor of the store stirred himself away from whatever it was he was doing behind the counter and walked in their direction.

"Can I help you folks?"

Jamie pointed to the window. "We want one of those ships."

Anne cautioned, "Maybe we'd better check the price. How much would one cost?"

The man considered the excitement in the little boy's face. "Ordinarily, quite a bit. I make 'em myself and don't like to part with 'em."

Jamie's face began to fall.

"But..." the man went on, "every once in a while I can be persuaded to let one go for less."

"How much?" Anne repeated, not sure of the man's intent. If he was merely stringing Jamie along, she wanted to put a quick end to the boy's hopes.

"How much you got?" the man asked.

Jamie dug in his pocket. He withdrew a curled-up five-dollar bill and a scattering of change. "This much," he said, holding it out.

Anne counted it. "Five dollars and eighty-five cents." She looked at the man.

His brow furrowed and he scratched his head. "What you goin' to do with it, son?"

"It's a present... for my daddy."

"Then five dollars and eighty-five cents it is. Which one do you want?"

Jamie hurried to the window display that was on clear view from inside the store. He examined the trio of sailing ships and finally picked the one that Anne knew had to be the most difficult to build because of the amount of the rigging. She whispered to the man, "Surely it costs more than that. I'll be happy to make up the difference."

"You the boy's mother?" he asked.

Anne experienced a funny sensation in her stomach, realizing that she would be very proud to say that she was. "No, just a friend."

The man shook his head. "Then the price stands. I don't get many little boys in my store. Especially little boys buying a present for their dad. I make the ships to pass my time. Not a lot goes on in this town, and I enjoy making 'em.''

He moved to pluck the ship from its position next to the other two ships. He brought it down and handed it to Jamie. "You probably want a card." He guided Jamie to the card selection.

Jamie looked to Anne for help. For the next ten minutes they stood before the cards, reading all the appropriate ones until Jamie finally settled on one with a comical dog pictured on the front.

"Card's on the house," the man surprised Anne by saying. Jamie accepted his generosity with an innocent "Thank you."

Because of the man's kindness, Anne looked around for something to give Robert herself. Jamie had been so excited during the drive into town, he would find it strange if she didn't contribute something to his father's special day. Also, she wanted to thank Robert. He had helped her more than once; it was the least she could do.

She looked around the store until she found a copy of an old sailing book. It had maps and gave pointers on sailing in a folksy, conversational style, and was originally printed in the latter part of the past century.

"How much is this?" she asked the proprietor.

He glanced at it. "Ten dollars."

"Surely it costs more than that," she protested.

"All it's worth to me is ten dollars. Is it worth that much to you?"

Anne reached into her purse for the money.

Just as the town was oddly sentimental, so did it seem were the inhabitants. But Overton had been such a town on the surface; warm to visitors, welcoming...

She thrust the thought from her mind. She couldn't continue to put people to the test. She had to learn to accept them as they were. Otherwise, the scar would grow until there was no flexibility left within her.

Thanking the man, she and Jamie left with their purchases. Jamie held the ship carefully, aware of its delicate rigging. He continued to hold it even when they found a drugstore that had a soda fountain, and they ordered two dishes of vanilla ice cream.

JAMIE WAS BOTH HAPPY and tired as Anne buckled him into his seat for the ride back to the cove. They chatted contentedly about this and that until, finally, Jamie gave a quiet little sigh and fell into a light sleep.

Anne glanced at him. His head was tilted to one side and his entire small body was relaxed—all but his hands, which were still clutching the ship.

She smiled softly to herself. Jamie was going to be quite something when he finished growing up. He already was quite something: fiercely loyal to those he cared for, with a budding sense of responsibility that sometimes wasn't found in persons ten times his age. Enthusiastic, humorous...he was an easy child to love.

Her fingers tightened on the wheel. She loved the boy. How could she deny it? He had come into her life when her emotions were at low ebb...reaching out to her, giving her the unconditional affection she had been searching for all her life. In *his* need, he had answered her own.

There was a major difficulty, though. Jamie and his father were short-time visitors to the Coast, just as she was. One day, very soon, they would each go their separate ways, probably never to see each other again.

One school of thought might say that it would have been better if she had never become close to the boy, or allowed him to become close to her. But then that school of thought was closed. It gave no latitude for emotions.

Anne glanced at Jamie again before redirecting her attention to the road. It was going to be hard to separate herself from him. Yet she didn't regret having taken him into her heart. She had received much more than she had given.

THE MAN RUBBED his thick neck. If anything, his cold had gotten worse. His head felt swollen, vastly enlarged. And the ache—if only the dull ache would go away. He coughed, a great phlegmy cough that racked his body and did little good.

That's what came of standing around in a cold night wind. How many times had his grandmother told him that? "You'll catch your death!" she had warned.

Funny, because that's exactly what had killed her. At seventy-five, she should have let some of the younger members of the family plan that last heist. Always a perfectionist, she had insisted on staking out the tiny firm that they knew was expecting a large delivery. The weather had turned bad…and so had she. She lived just long enough to congratulate them on their success.

He coughed again and transferred his hand to his chest. It hurt like hell when he did that. He was probably coming down with pneumonia.

If only the woman would hurry. Then he could finish the job and stretch out in a nice warm bed. The thought was almost a physical ache.

He forced himself to sit straighter and narrow his watery eyes on the horizon. When he saw her car come around the bend, it would be time to start his own. He had planned everything, down to his statement of horror and denial: he had been on his side of the road, but the other car's driver had panicked, suddenly jerking the wheel in the wrong direction . . .

A car plunging off a narrow cliff road was all too common on the California coast.

ANNE'S BODY WAS TENSE as she negotiated the curving roadway. This was certainly not her favorite place to drive. A two-lane highway hugging a cut in the earth where a road had been forged—one side next to a cliff and the other side, her side, a direct one-hundred-foot plunge to the crashing sea and rocks below. There was no shoulder to speak of, so she was somewhat relieved that there were few, if any, oncoming vehicles. She had hated driving it on her first trip to the beach house and hated it equally now. The one plus was that the view was magnificent . . . if a person was willing to take her life in her hands to look!

She kept her gaze firmly on the road ahead. She would take no chances with her fate or with Jamie's.

THE ENGINE CAUGHT and was gunned into unwilling life. Slowly, the car moved out onto the road, away from the tiny lay-by. Little by little it picked up speed. The face of the man behind the wheel was set in determination.

ANNE SAW THE CAR coming and even though she knew there was really no need to fear, her heart gave a little jump. So far, she had met no one on the narrow road, and she had wished to keep it that way. But the car was old and seemed to be keeping to its allotted side. Whoever was driving it had probably traveled this stretch of highway so many times that it had become old hat. Still she kept a wary eye.

Her car was climbing steadily, striving for the summit of the set of hills that separated the beach house from the fishing village. It was a gradual climb, but it added to the tension of the moment.

Anne glanced at the oncoming car. It was still some distance away. She glanced at the drop-off on the other side and swallowed tightly. She was glad that Jamie was asleep; if he had still been chattering she would have had to ask him to stop. She needed all her concentration right now.

The other car was nearing. She adjusted her hands on the steering wheel, trying for a better grip. The action hadn't been necessary, but it made her feel better. She felt the muscles in her back tighten.

As she had thought, it was an older car, and a big one. It seemed to take up much more of the road than was its due. It was almost as bad as meeting a truck!

Anne's muscles contracted even more. She scrupulously stayed to her portion of the road. Her car was not moving very fast, but she wished that she could slow it further. Only if she did, the road's incline would make restarting the climb difficult.

The other car was almost directly across from her, and for some reason, Anne glanced into it, her eyes skipping to the driver. In a split second she saw that he was a big man, close to middle age, with a kind of blurry look, yet with an expression set in antagonism and eyes that bored into her coldly. When he saw her looking at him, he smiled...and the chill sank deeply into Anne's bones.

There was no time to gasp, no time to look away. With horror, she saw him turn his steering wheel sharply, trying to force his car into hers...to drive her off the cliff and into the sea.

Anne's reaction was instantaneous. Born of collected fear, her responses were keen. She shifted down a gear and rammed her foot all the way down on the accelerator—it was her only chance. If the car remained where it was, it would be hit.

Anne loved the car for its look—sleek and smooth and stylish. But it also had a powerful engine that was capable of reacting swiftly. Like something shot from a catapult, it jumped forward, its tires instantly catching on the road surface, giving a high-pitched little squeal, but not wasting time or energy in a loud screech.

Anne's heart was in her throat as they shot forward. She sensed Jamie come awake in the seat next to her, but she didn't spare him a glance. She was waiting for the sound of an impact...waiting for the push that would send them careening to their deaths.

No impact came. There was only power. The car was lunging crazily forward—a fact she had to correct or she would send them over the cliff herself. She eased off the accelerator, but only enough to regain control. Then her eyes jerked to the rearview mirror. She saw that the large car had slewed into her lane, and that the driver was now having to fight to keep himself on the roadway.

Anne didn't watch any longer. They had escaped. At least for the moment. But for how long would their safety last? Until the car righted itself and found a place to turn around?

They continued to shoot forward. For the moment, Anne no longer feared the road. Her fear centered on getting away. She negotiated the remaining turns of the narrow roadway like a race driver, using her ability, using the car's maneuverability.

"Anne?" Jamie questioned.

Anne shook her head, silently telling the boy to wait. He held tightly as the car moved forward, his eyes wide, his face white with strain. Only the seat belt kept him from being thrown about.

Finally, they reached the summit where the road straightened and moved away from the cliff line.

Anne glanced in the rearview mirror. There was no other car in sight. Still, she didn't rest on her laurels. With her lips tightly held, she kept the car moving swiftly...eventually passing up the turn that would take them to the beach house and moving on to the lane to the cottage.

Her body was starting to tremble now. She felt that they were almost safe. Somehow...by some miracle...they had made it.

She braked the car to a stop in a cloud of sand causing it to slide sideways off the drive. Before it fully ceased motion, she jumped out and hurried to Jamie's door. Her hands fumbled with the handle.

Jamie unlatched his seat belt and helped her with the door. When she reached in to scoop him into her arms, he made no protest, but protected the wooden ship as best he could. The entire ride it had been in his hands. He had kept it safe.

Tears were streaking down Anne's cheeks as she ran. Her feet tangled in the sand at first, her ankles turning. But she didn't notice any pain—at least, not that she paid any heed to. She hurried toward the door, which was pulled open just as she got to it.

Robert stood in the doorway, his expression a puzzled study before he absorbed Anne's state of terror and Jamie's equally white face. He hurried them inside, closing the door behind them and then locking it.

Anne did not put Jamie down. She continued to hold him, her breaths coming in jagged jerks.

"What happened?" Robert demanded.

For a moment, she couldn't answer him. Jamie squirmed in her arms until she let him down. But she kept a hand on his shoulder, trying to assure herself with his presence.

"We—someone tried to run us off the road."

"Where?"

"The road"—she was panting—"the road along the cliff."

Jamie made an inarticulate cry and broke free of Anne's hold to run to his father. Robert went down on one knee to enfold the unsettled little boy in his arms. All the while he looked at Anne.

She knew that both of them were thinking the same thing. Her body continued to tremble.

Jamie moved in his father's arms to glance around at Anne. He freed an arm and reached out to her, including her in the tiny group.

Anne remained still for a moment, her mind reeling with the import of what had just happened. No longer could she put the accidents down to happenstance. The man had meant to kill her—them! There was no debate left in the fact. He had meant, coldbloodedly, to kill them.

She gave a small sob and dropped to her knees on the floor beside the boy and his father. Because of her, the boy had almost died.

Keeping one arm around his son, Robert placed his other arm around Anne. He held them both until their tears dried and they pushed away.

Robert studied Jamie, taking in the tear-blotched face. He wasn't sure if the boy had been afraid or if he was reflecting the fear he sensed in Anne.

He stood up, catching his son into his arms, balancing him on his hip. Anne got to her feet as well, smoothing down her skirt, rubbing at her cheeks to erase the traces of moisture.

"Do you think it was an accident?" he asked.

Anne bit her lip and shook her head.

Robert's heart chilled as he visualized the car sliding off the cliff road, and an impotent anger took hold of him.

Anne saw his look and immediately stiffened. He thought she was at fault. He was blaming her for what had happened.

"I didn't mean..." she started to stammer. "I didn't..."

Robert frowned.

"I would never have brought Jamie if..." She caught at her lip, trying to stem the new tide of tears.

"I know that," he clipped.

"Everything was fine until we got on the cliff road. Then a big car came. I saw the man. He...he..."

Jamie made a small sound, drawing the attention of the adults. "Don't cry, Anne," he whispered brokenly. "Don't cry. It's not your fault."

Robert patted his son's arm. "Let's sit down, okay? I think we all need to."

Anne's body was rigid when she tried unsuccessfully to move. She watched as Robert lowered Jamie to the couch and looked back for her. She shook her head, denying her desire to follow. He sat down at his son's side.

"It's no one's fault," he said, looking at Anne as well as his child. "What's this?" he asked the boy, touching the sailing ship his son was still clutching. One of the smaller masts had broken in the ordeal and when Jamie saw the damage, he started to wail.

"It's broken!" he cried.

"Nothing that can't be fixed with a little glue," Robert reassured him. Inside himself, his stomach plunged. A wooden ship could be repaired; a life, once lost, could not.

"It's for your birthday," Jamie cried again, not mollified.

Robert took the ship from his son's hands. He examined it carefully, including the snapped mast. "What a beauty!" he complimented. "Where did you find it?" He wanted to get his son's mind from the terror he had experienced. He saw that Anne had now recovered to the point where she was thinking again and would know what he was doing. They would talk privately as soon as they could. There was no use in frightening Jamie further.

"In town. A man made it. He makes lots of ships, but I thought this one was the best."

Robert touched the hanging rigging. "Do you know where the glue is?"

Jamie nodded.

"Then why don't you go get it and we'll have this like new in no time."

With a solemn little face Jamie jumped from the couch and did as his father instructed.

Anne wished *she* could disappear. She wished that she had picked any other spot on the coast but this one to come to after her experience in Overton.

She looked away from Robert's steady gaze.

"Are you all right?" he asked quietly after a few seconds had passed.

"Yes," she breathed, still feeling the censure of his emotions.

"How did you get away?" he asked.

She twisted her hands together. She didn't want to think about what had happened, but knew that the thoughts would not stop—not for some time. "I saw what he was about to do and got us out of there."

"You must have quick reflexes."

She nodded. "Look . . . I'm sorry. I didn't mean to get Jamie involved in all of this."

"You didn't think that there was anything to involve him in."

"I was stupid."

"You just didn't want to believe the worst. I don't blame you. No one would."

"I should have been more careful."

"Sounds to me like you were. You're both here now."

"I should never have come here!" she cried. "I should never have..."

"The past can't be changed."

Sudden anger lighted her eyes. "He meant to do it. I saw his face!"

"Did you recognize him? Have you seen him before?"

"No, but I'd recognize him if I ever saw him again. He—" she shivered "—I can't get his face out of my mind!"

"What are you going to do?"

Anne faced the abyss. "I don't know."

"I think you should stay here for the night."

When she thought of going back to the beach house and staying there alone, she knew she didn't want to do that. She looked away. "Haven't I already caused you enough trouble?"

Robert stood up and crossed to her stiffly held body. He reached out to grasp her shoulders and make her turn to face him. "For the last time, this is not your fault. We're involved because whoever's trying to kill you has involved us."

"You wouldn't have to stay involved."

Robert smiled slightly. "I don't think we should talk about this any more right now. Everyone's too upset. In a while, we'll go over to your place and you can get some things together."

Jamie came back into the room, carrying the bottle of glue. "This is all I could find. Is it okay?"

Robert moved away from Anne. "It's perfect," he said, lifting the bottle to look at it.

Anne watched as he patiently glued the mast back together. Her eyes moved over his tall, lean form. In the midst of her fear, she had passed up the drive to the beach house and instead, frantically hurried to the cottage. Subconsciously, was she searching for human succor? Or subconsciously, was she rushing to only one person—Robert—because he had a way of making things seem more manageable, even when they weren't?

She was getting too close to this family.

ANNE WAS QUIET as they trudged the short distance back to the cottage. Robert was at her side, carrying her suitcase, and Jamie had already skipped far ahead of them, playing one of his made-up games that involved his complete attention.

"Have you decided what you're going to do?" Robert asked, breaking the silence.

She shrugged. "I still don't have any proof. It wouldn't do any good to go to the police."

"I'd already thought of that."

She nodded. Then, squaring her shoulders, she voiced the thought that had been circling in her mind all the while she packed. "I think the only way to solve this...is to go back to Overton."

Robert didn't respond at first. Finally he surprised her by saying, "Maybe you're right."

The idea picked up energy. "If I do that, maybe then I can find out who's behind all of this and why."

"Sounds logical. You don't expect to be welcomed back, do you?"

"No."

"What's Overton like?"

"How do you mean?"

"How far away is it?"

"About a hundred or so miles."

"Which way?"

"East, of course."

He laughed, the first laughter she had heard since her and Jamie's precipitous arrival. "I didn't think it was west—in the Ocean. I meant, north...south...?"

"Sort of south."

"Do you still have a place there?"

"Yes, for the time being."

They walked on, to the accompaniment of the waves rushing onto the shore.

She was going to miss the sound of the sea, miss Jamie, miss— She pulled her thoughts back, impatient with where they were going. Robert had turned out to be a nice man, a kind man...someone far different from the person she had thought him to be at first. He was wholly human, pulled by conflicting emotions just as she was. That was all there was to it. She might think of him from time to time, but that was all.

"I'm going with you."

The words settled on the wind. At first she wasn't sure if she had heard them correctly. She glanced at him, frowning. "What?"

"I'm going with you."

She shook her head. "No. You can't. I don't want you to come."

"*I* want to."

"No!"

They stopped walking and turned to face each other.

"This has nothing to do with you!" she protested.

"I think it does. Whoever is after you almost killed my son, remember?"

"It's a little hard to forget...of course I remember!"

"Then it's settled."

"No, it's not settled. What will you do with Jamie? You can't bring him into something like this."

"I'll take him back to his mother. He'll understand, especially when I tell him that I'm helping you."

"I won't let you!"

"You can't stop me. What kind of person do you think I am? I can't just let you go off and confront something like this on your own."

"I'm perfectly capable."

"Two people can watch each other's backs. One can't. One always has to face away from a wall...and you can never be too sure about the wall."

"Am I sure of you?" she challenged.

"You can be sure I'm not going to kill you."

"I still can't let you do it. What if something happened?"

"I'm not totally without experience. The areas of the world I've been stationed in aren't exactly known for their stability. I can take care of myself."

"But what about Jamie?"

"I'll call Karen first thing in the morning."

"I don't mean that...what if something happens to you?"

"Nothing will."

"You don't know that."

"A person doesn't know if he's going to have a heart attack getting out of bed in the morning, either. I love my boy. I'll do anything for him. But what kind of a father would I be if I never did anything because I might get hurt? Anyway, you're the one in trouble. Not me."

"Whoever it is might feel threatened by you, too."

He smiled suddenly. "Good, I hope so."

Anne turned away from him. For the moment, she was out of arguments.

ROBERT WASN'T QUITE as cavalier about his insistence on accompanying her as he wanted Anne to believe. He had thought the problem through carefully, examining every plus and every minus. He knew the situation could be dangerous, but he frequently lived with danger. A threat to his own life had ceased to faze him.

But a threat to someone else, a threat that also involved his son, did.

He didn't want to bring Jamie back to Karen so soon. They still had almost two weeks left of their time together. And retrieving the remaining two weeks at a later date would probably be difficult. But how could he let Anne go off on her own?

He slid a glance toward her that was anything but casual and yet would have passed for just that if caught.

He wanted to help her. And it wasn't merely as a male chauvinist assisting a helpless woman. She wasn't helpless and he wasn't a chauvinist—at least, neither of them would have admitted the flaw. It was something more: he cared about what happened to her.

Robert continued to walk in silence. Caring. Long ago his father had tried to explain to him about caring. Why—after each marriage had broken up—he had kept the children. But he had been too immature then to understand. He thought his father was a weak man. Now, he wasn't so sure...at least not in every way. Maybe he had more of his father in him than he thought. He cared about his son and he cared about Anne. Not in the same way, of course. He loved Jamie. And Anne—?

He couldn't call what he felt for her love. She was a woman who needed his help.

Only...how many women had he helped in his lifetime if there wasn't some kind of payback? Yet he expected no payback from Anne. None at all. Maybe a simple thank you and a let's keep in touch.

Again he pictured the car she and Jamie were riding in plunging over the side of the cliff to the ocean below. It was anger he felt. Pure anger...directed toward the person who was responsible.

Only anger didn't have a softer side. And when he looked at Anne, softness was almost all he felt.

He gave a short, impatient sigh.

She heard it and glanced at him, but he kept his gaze firmly on the beach ahead.

Chapter Eight

The telephone was ringing as he entered the hall. Quick steps took him to the office door, but haste made him fumble with the key. It took him three tries to get the door open. Finally, exasperated and afraid that the phone would stop ringing, he dashed into his set of offices. His hello was gruff, breathless.

"It's me," came the voice from the other end of the line.

The man sank into his chair, his body tensed for what he hoped he was about to hear.

"It ain't finished yet," was what he heard.

An icy fear spread through his stomach. His hand adjusted itself on the receiver, sudden moisture making it clammy. He took refuge in anger. "Why the hell not?"

There was a small silence. "She keeps slipping through."

"You let her slip through! That's not what I'm paying you for!"

"I ain't seen much of that yet."

"Which is a good thing. I won't pay for inefficiency."

"She's got some man she's hanging around."

"So?"

"So it makes an accident a little harder to arrange." The sentence was cut off by a racking cough.

The man in the business suit gritted his teeth. "Maybe it's just that you're not very good. Maybe I should find someone who is."

The snuffling sound of a nose being blown and wiped came from the line. "Maybe you should just do that. Only I want the rest of my money."

"For what?" the man exploded. "You haven't done anything!"

"For expenses."

"I won't give you a penny more!"

"Maybe you should just think about that. You're not exactly in a position to have the word put out on the street."

"Are you threatening me?"

Another racking cough. "I think I should get something out of this besides pneumonia!"

The man in the business suit calculated the odds. He decided to bluff. "Get lost, loser."

Then he hung up.

For moments afterward, he stared at the silent phone, wondering if he had made the correct decision.

ROBERT REPLACED THE RECEIVER, a mixture of emotions marking his expression. He hadn't expected that. Karen didn't want him to bring Jamie back yet. She was having too many troubles of her own—with her husband, with her pregnancy. In fact, she told him, she had been going to call to ask if Jamie could stay with him for another few weeks...the baby should be delivered by then and things settled back to normal.

Robert stared blankly at the wall across from him. He didn't know how to react. Part of him was angry with her. She had even refused when he told her that bringing Jamie with him would be extremely difficult, even dangerous.

Yet, long ago, hadn't he used the same argument to absolve himself from guilt at leaving his newborn son? Could he blame her for not believing him this time?

Karen was having a difficult time herself. She was under a lot of tension. Bryce Jennings was not an easy man to live with. But he had been Karen's choice...and it was his child that she was carrying.

What really made him angry, though, was her intimation that Bryce would be even more difficult if Jamie came back ahead of schedule.

Robert ached to say to hell with both of them. He wanted to plaster Jennings to a wall and punish him for the punishment he had already meted out to Jamie. He wanted to force Karen to take better care of the boy, to make her see how Jamie was paying for the turmoil in their lives.

But he found himself embroiled in a strange compassion for her. At the moment she was doing the best she could. There were too many conflicting pressures in her life that were pulling in opposite directions. He knew that she loved Jamie and wanted the best for him. Yet, conversely, she also loved her husband. The situation didn't bode well for their future, and she had to know that.

Once, not long ago, Robert would have found a measure of satisfaction in her quandary. They hadn't parted on the most amiable of terms...hell, they hadn't married on them either. Karen had been three months pregnant, and he had been caught in an obligation to duty that grated at his immaturity.

Yet, now, he could not gloat. He saw how the problems one person faced affected the lives of everyone around them. In small ways, in large ways...in every way. Everyone was interdependent, links in a chain. If one link became frayed, the chain weakened.

Karen. Anne. Jamie and himself.

Robert absently ran a hand down his thigh. He didn't want to bring the boy to Overton...but did he have a choice?

ANNE LOOKED UP from the newspaper she was reading. She still avoided the front section, unable to read the trials and tribulations of other people who might be just as innocent as she was and yet were caught up in situations far beyond their control.

Robert came into the room to take a seat at the table across from her. Jamie was in his room, straightening it. Robert had already told him that he was going to go back to his mother sooner than expected because Anne needed his help. Jamie had wanted to help, too, but Robert had refused the offer. The boy had been quiet after that, going to his room without protest.

Robert fiddled with a spoon that had been left on the table. Eventually, he said, "She won't take him back right now."

Anne laid the newspaper aside.

He went on, "She says she can't. I believe her."

Anne was momentarily silent, but then said, "I'll go back to Overton on my own. It's okay. I can do it. That's what I'd rather do anyway."

Robert shook his head emphatically. "No. We'll all go."

"But we can't take Jamie!"

"He'll be all right."

"How can you say that?" she demanded.

"I'll take care of him."

"While you take care of me. What do you think you are? Some kind of superman?"

"The boy will be fine. So will you."

"I don't like it."

"You don't have to. Just look upon us as friendly leeches."

He smiled slightly at his lame joke, but it was easy to see that he wasn't wholly pleased with the situation, either.

Anne stopped her protest, because no matter how many times she might proclaim her ability to take complete care of herself, she had been braced by the thought of Robert's company.

As the time approached, the malevolence waiting for her in Overton loomed larger in her mind. The people would not be happy to see her back. Neither would the person who was trying to have her killed.

JAMIE WAS THRILLED by the turn of events. As far as Anne and Robert knew, he didn't suspect the real reason for their trip to Overton. Robert told him only that his mother had given her permission for him to come, and he spent most of the trip with his face glued to one of the side windows, watching what he could see of the vista ahead.

As they neared Overton, Anne's tension increased. The terrain and billboard advertisements called out to her as a return to both the familiar and the frightful. They were driving Robert's rental car...it would be less conspicuous than her own, he had explained.

Then she began to see old faces. But no one recognized her. She had left town on her own; she was returning with a family.

She directed Robert to the home she had used her inheritance to buy upon her arrival in Overton. It sat a short distance back from the street, surrounded by a neat white fence. Once it had been pretty, cared for. Now, the yard she had tended in her spare time was dying from lack of watering, and what flowers there were left were wilted and sad-looking.

On the front door remained the vestiges of smashed eggs, the drippings frozen in silent reproach. Her mailbox was dented and off its hinges, listing to one side. The screens on her windows were marked with soap and torn. One screen was absent entirely and the window broken.

Anne looked away from the carnage. Robert sat with his arms crossed over the steering wheel, his eyes hooded. Jamie mouthed a silent "Wow."

"Well," she said. "That's home!" Her words were tight, emotion-clogged, even as they tried to sound flippant.

Robert opened his door to get out. When Anne did the same, Jamie jumped out on her side. The three of them stood at the gate.

"Looks like someone had a little fun," Robert murmured.

"Most of it was like this when I left." She motioned to the broken window. "That wasn't, though."

"Be prepared for what you find inside," Robert warned.

Anne tensed. It would only stand to reason. Just because she left town didn't mean that the townspeople's spleen was truly vented. Some might wish to take their anger out on her house. It was a wonder the place was still standing.

Her fingers tightened on the key as they approached the front door. She inserted it in the lock and turned. The door swung open.

Just as she suspected the interior of the house had been trashed. Graffiti was scrawled on the walls, garbage was strewn on the floor. Her furniture had been tossed about; some of it broken.

In the kitchen everything had been pulled from the cabinets and smashed. Pots and pans looked as if they had been used to pound against the counters. Cleansers had been spread on the floor. The curtains had been torn from their hooks.

The rest of the house had received little better treatment. There were only two bedrooms and one bath—and none of them were usable.

Anne was crying silently by the time they had finished the circuit, Jamie's hand held tightly in her own.

"What happened?" Jamie asked, awed. He had never seen anything like it before. "Somethin' explode?"

Robert took the necessity of an answer away from Anne. His lips were tight as he said, "Some people were angry at Anne. They took it out on her house."

Jamie looked back at him with wide eyes. "They weren't very nice people."

"No," Robert agreed. He looked at Anne. Her shoulders were hunched, tears were rolling down her cheeks. She looked momentarily defeated. A great anger welled up inside him. That someone could be so vicious to her! It made him want to find them and...

Instead of giving in to his anger, he placed an arm gently around her shoulders. She didn't try to push him away. Rather, she turned to him, needing his presence, needing his assurance.

Robert experienced an odd sensation. It was as if she were a part of him. He knew exactly what she was feeling...how hard it was for her even to lift her head.

Her hazel eyes, dulled with an unbelievable hurt, looked up at him as she whispered, "Do you see? Do you see why I left?"

Robert wanted to make things right for her. But there was nothing he could do. He motioned toward the graffiti. "It was probably kids."

"Does that matter?" she demanded tightly. "The hate comes from the same place."

"It looks as if it got out of hand. Maybe things are different now."

She shook her head.

Robert looked at the room again. "Does this town have some sort of hotel? We certainly can't stay here...not until we clean the place up."

Anne straightened, pushing her hair away from her face as she tried to control her vacillating emotions.

One part of her wanted to run away again, as far and as fast as she could. The other part was experiencing a surging anger. She would not allow herself to become a victim again. They had done it to her once; they would not do it to her again.

"There's a motel, but it's not very big."

"All we need is a couple of rooms."

"Don't use my name."

Robert smiled dryly, "I won't."

ANNE WAITED IN THE CAR with Jamie as Robert registered them at the motel. When the attendant briefly glanced out the wide window that overlooked the motel's entrance, she covered her appearance by turning her face away and pretending to fluff her hair in the visor mirror.

Robert came back to the car. "That's done," he said, slipping into position behind the wheel. "We're in E-3 and -4."

"How did you register us?" Anne asked.

He didn't hesitate to answer. "As Mr. and Mrs. Singleton and son. They're connecting rooms."

Anne nodded. It was the logical thing to do.

Robert started the car. Jamie watched the proceedings quietly from the back seat. But all at once he sat forward to point. "They have a pool!" he cried.

Anne and Robert located the postage-stamp-size pool at the same time.

"Sure do, sport," Robert agreed.

"Can we go for a swim, Daddy?"

"We'll see, son. I can't make any promises."

Jamie lapsed into silence.

THE ROOMS WERE COMFORTABLE, if not perfectly cared for. The motel was old and showing its age. The bathrooms needed new fixtures, and the walls could have used a fresh coat of paint. But the beds weren't lumpy beneath their nondescript covers and the pillows were soft.

Jamie informed them about the pillows immediately after trying one out. His father had moved their things into one room and Anne's into the other.

She stood in the doorway that separated them. "What do we do now? Have you thought about it?"

Robert straightened from putting away some of his and Jamie's clothing. "I think the only thing we can do is get you seen around town."

Anne swallowed.

He noted her reaction and explained, "I know it will be hard, but otherwise there's no use in us coming here. We have to flush the man out." He was careful not to say the word killer in front of Jamie.

Anne was equally circumspect. "How will we know him?"

"We won't...probably not for a while."

"So in the meantime...?"

"We just act normally."

She gave a tinny laugh. "Normally?"

"We'll start by cleaning up your house. Whoever it is will eventually tip his hand."

Anne turned away, closing the door between the rooms. At the moment she needed to be alone.

ANNE HELD HER HEAD HIGH as they walked up and down the aisles in the grocery store. Everyone was looking at them...at her...and she could sense their dumbfounded amazement.

Various cleansers were in their shopping basket along with a broom, a mop and a dustpan. On the way to the store they had stopped at her house—a second viewing didn't improve matters—and made a list of the things they would need.

When they neared the checkout stand, Jamie noticed a gum-ball machine positioned close by. He examined the prizes that could be won and hurried to his father's side to ask for change.

The proprietor of the store had positioned himself behind the register, having taken over from the regular clerk as soon as he spotted Anne.

His burly arms were crossed and he had a set expression on his face as he said, "Your money's not good in this store, Miss Reynolds."

Anne paused in putting the cleansers on the conveyer belt. "It's regulation US issue, Mr. Thompson."

"It could be gold, for all I care. I don't want your sort shopping in my store."

Robert merged into the conversation. His pale eyes were narrowed as he looked across at the man. For the first time, Anne sensed an element of danger in him, as if he did know very well how to take care of himself.

"I'd advise you to rethink your position," he said softly.

"I don't have to serve anyone I don't want to. And I don't want to serve her. Who the hell are you, anyway?"

"I'm her lawyer."

The quietly worded claim worked wonders, just as Robert wished it to. Immediately the proprietor began to back down, blustering as he went. Like most businessmen, he didn't relish being dragged into court.

"I still don't see... This is America, for God's sake!" But all the time he was protesting, he was reaching for products, ringing them up. "People have rights here."

Robert collected Jamie, holding him close to his side. The boy was examining the prize he had won along with a gum ball. As he chewed the sweet treat, he seemed oblivious to what was happening around them. But Robert wasn't. He felt the censure of the other customers, the grumbles of protest as the grocer caved in to pressure.

Anne paid for her purchases and collected the bag while Robert picked up the larger objects.

"We'd like a receipt," Robert said.

The man gave it to him with aggrieved malice.

As they left the store, a hum of voices followed them.

"YOU LIED TO HIM," Anne whispered so that Jamie couldn't hear. They were in the car, driving toward her house.

"It worked."

"Yes, but..."

"In my job, the truth doesn't always get you what you need. People respond better to what they *want* to hear... or to what they *don't want* to hear. I've gotten many a story by bending reality a bit."

Anne was silent.

He glanced at her. "I don't like to lie to people. I wish life were perfect. I wish there weren't despots intent on having their own way. I wish people didn't have to be pushed into doing the right thing...but sometimes they do. And sometimes a person has to fight them on their own level."

"Doesn't it ever bother you?"

"Of course it does...sometimes. Other times, like right now, I'm not bothered a bit about what happened. I think the man deserved exactly what he got. Would you have preferred me to hit him?"

Anne's face relaxed into a slow smile. "Possibly."

Robert smiled back. "Ah-ha! The lady prefers violence."

Anne's smile broadened. She laughed. "Not really. Only sometimes."

"And here I was thinking that you clung to a higher moral plane than a mere reporter."

"I thought what you did was wonderful."

"It did get him moving, didn't it?"

Anne laughed again and Robert was pleased to hear the sound.

THE RUMOR THAT ANNE REYNOLDS had returned to Overton swept through the town like wildfire. Telephones rang. Hushed voices conferred. People stopped on street corners to talk. Few of them could believe it. She had come back? The woman must be a glutton for punishment. Of all the nerve. Did she think their memories were so short? Barely a month had passed.

Feelings still ran high as the aftermath of Kinkaid Systems' closing continued to be felt throughout the tiny community. Everyone was financially hurting and afraid that they were going to hurt much more. It could be the end of Overton. Some people had already packed and moved away.

THEY STARTED IN THE KITCHEN. In the beginning the mess looked overwhelming. But as the hours passed, they could see the results of their labors. Even Jamie was proud of what he had accomplished—replacing all the scattered canned goods in the pantry.

Robert stood back from the wall where he had been trying to remove graffiti from the paper. "I'm afraid this is a total loss. It's going to have to be replaced."

Anne nodded. She straightened from scrubbing the last section of the kitchen floor. "I thought it would."

"Are you any good at hanging wallpaper?"

"I've never tried."

"It's a pain. I did it once a long time ago...I've tried to forget the experience."

Anne surveyed the room. One out of six, plus a hall. If they kept going at this pace, they would have everything cleaned in a week. If they were given a week.

"I'm hungry," Robert announced. "Is anyone else?"

Jamie hopped across the room. "I am!"

They both looked at Anne. She glanced around the immediate area. It was clean, but she didn't know exactly what was left in her cupboard to prepare. "I don't—" she started to say when Robert cut her off.

"We're going out to eat. This town does have a restaurant, doesn't it?"

"Yes—" she answered hesitantly.

"Don't worry. They'll serve us."

Anne looked down at her clothing. "I want to change."

"I think we all do. Sport, why don't you help me board up the front window while Anne finishes in here."

Jamie skipped out of the room at his father's side.

As ROBERT NAILED a series of flat boards across the broken window, Jamie played with his shoelaces, waiting for him to finish. He tied a knot, then another knot. He loved to tie knots.

"Daddy," he asked after a short time had passed. "Why didn't that man want Anne to shop in his store?"

Robert paused in his work to look at his son. "What do you think?"

"Because he's one of the people who don't like her?"

Robert nodded and Jamie frowned.

"But . . . she's nice! Why don't they like her?"

"Because she had to do something that hurt a lot of the people who live here."

"What kind of something?"

"Do you know what a trial is?"

"Like on TV?"

Robert wondered what kind of shows his son watched. Children pick up so much more than what parents give them credit for. "Like on TV," he confirmed. "Anne had to tell something about some men who live in this town . . . something the people living here didn't want her to say. What she said helped put those men in jail."

"Were they bad men?" Jamie asked, his face serious with his question.

"In their own way."

"Was what she said the truth?"

"Yes."

"Then she did the right thing. Mommy always says telling the truth is the right thing."

Robert gave silent thanks to his ex-wife. As he told Anne, he sometimes had been forced into bending the truth, but he didn't want his son to have to do that. Especially not until he could see the difference between an outright lie and a bluff.

"Your mother was right."

"But I heard you tell a lie."

Robert sighed. He didn't think the boy had heard. He went down on his haunches beside him. "Jamie...look at me."

Jamie did.

"What I did, I did for Anne. I told you I had to help her."

"Yeah—"

Robert closed his eyes. This was getting difficult. How could he make the boy see that he valued the truth even as he sometimes used falsehoods? "I couldn't let the man be mean to Anne. He has no reason to be. I made him afraid that he would get into trouble if he wasn't nice to her. Do you understand?"

"Yeah—"

Robert rubbed his neck. Being a father was hard work.

Jamie looked at him in all innocence, and asked, "Is it kind of like telling someone you like something when you really don't just because that's all they have and you don't want to be mean?''

The logic was convoluted but accurate. Robert heaved a great mental sigh when he agreed, "Yeah—exactly like that.''

Jamie broke into a grin. "That's okay then! Mommy says that isn't a lie. She says it's a fib. And fibs like that don't count.''

Anne entered the room at that moment. She was drying her hands on a paper towel but stopped when she saw them.

Jamie jumped to his feet. "Anne! Daddy didn't lie! It was a fib—and fibs like that don't count!''

Robert glanced at her and shrugged lightly. His face held a blend of consternation and sheepish satisfaction.

When the boy ran to her to hug her around the legs, she smoothed his hair, her eyes still on Robert.

"That's what his mother told him,'' he explained.

"Oh,'' Anne murmured. For the first time, hearing the boy's mother mentioned caused an invisible knife to pierce her heart. Both for the boy...and for his father.

BOLD AS BRASS, the man walked into the city government offices. He knew where to go; he had been there once before. He didn't stop until he was at the correct office. A receptionist tried to stop him, but he paid her no mind. With his bull-like body, he plowed ahead.

The well-dressed man sitting behind the gray metal desk jumped when he saw who had thundered into his office. His face flushed, then immediately paled. For a moment, he looked panicked; then, retrieving his aggressive persona, he launched into a verbal attack.

"What do you think you're doing? You have no business coming here!"

"I want my money!" the man bellowed.

"Close the door."

"You close the door!"

The man in the business suit stalked across the room. He closed the door carefully, although what he wanted to do was slam it off its hinges.

"All right," he hissed, forcing calmness as he turned. "Now explain."

"I want my money!" the intruder repeated.

"You've already got all you're going to get. I thought I made that clear!"

"You didn't make anything clear. You hung up."

"And your feelings are hurt?" the other man sneered.

The burly man didn't wait to react. He took two large steps across the small room and jerked the man up against the wall. "You're gonna give me what you owe. Either that or I tell everyone what you did."

"I haven't done anything...because you haven't done your job."

"You hired me!"

"Who's going to believe that?"

The large man frowned. His grandmother would tell him that he had been a fool. Get it all up front, she had always said. Get everything in the beginning, because you don't know how a job's going to go, she had said; and she was right. Normally, he operated that way. But this time his employer had been so afraid, so determined . . . and adamant that he would only pay half. And his cold had been coming on.

His damned cold. It had to have been that that kept getting in the way of his doing his job properly. He gave the man a shake, causing his head to wobble.

A shy tapping sounded on the door. Both men froze. The tapping came again. "Mr. Elliot?" a reedy masculine voice questioned.

His assistant! Randall Elliot had never been so glad to hear the man's voice before. He vowed he would make up for all the times he had cursed his aid's perseverance to a problem.

"Yes?" he croaked. "Yes . . . what is it?"

The door started to open and Randall Elliot was released from his position against the wall. When he was on his own two feet again, he straightened his tie and loosened his shoulder muscles. The man could have killed him!

Peter Martin stepped into the room, his mouse-like eyes flitting from his boss to the large man at his side. The intruder looked to be snarling. "I'm sorry to interrupt," Peter apologized meekly. "I didn't know you had a visitor."

"My visitor is just going," Randall Elliot replied.

The large man glowered at both men, but he saved his best look for his one-time employer. "You remember what I said. If the money isn't in my hands by the end of the day, I call the newspapers."

Then he stomped from the room.

Randall Elliot burned with embarrassment. He didn't like to be made to look bad in front of a subordinate. He reverted to type, climbing back into his over-glorified dignity at the same time as he resumed his seat at the desk.

"Yes, Martin. How can I help you?"

Peter Martin laughed inside himself. So the boss was in some sort of trouble. It served him right. He wished he hadn't interrupted. "About the MacIntire account . . ."

Chapter Nine

The restaurant boasted few patrons. Many tables and chairs were empty; only one waitress worked the floor.

As had happened in the grocery store, conversation immediately halted upon their arrival and all eyes turned to watch them as they made their way to a booth.

Jamie slid to the middle section, happily unaware of what was happening. Anne, wholly aware, followed him to her seat, while Robert positioned himself on the cushion across from her.

His pale eyes swept over the people who were still looking at them. Some of them turned away, others didn't. To those, he gave a short nod, which finally caused them to shift their attention elsewhere.

"Warm, friendly people," he murmured.

"They can be," Anne returned. "They were."

The waitress moved past them, her gaze centered determinedly on a man seated in the booth next to them. She was carrying a beaker of coffee. When she passed them again, as if they were invisible, Robert's hand came out to grasp her arm, surprising her, causing her to turn.

"We'd like some coffee, please. And some orange soda for the boy. And a menu."

The waitress's young face was stiff. Anne remembered that her name was Mary. She had come into the print shop two months earlier, to order wedding invitations, and had been very happy with the results. She had even given one to Anne—who couldn't help wondering, ironically, if the invitation still held. Probably not. Obviously not, from the accusing glance the young girl threw at her before answering.

"I'm going off duty. You'll have to find someone else."

Robert smiled. "A few seconds longer won't hurt."

The girl's face twisted. "I won't serve her!"

"Why not?"

"Hello, Mary." Anne tried smiling, too. The girl had been shy and sweet and all wrapped up in her wedding the last time she had seen her. It was hard to believe she could have changed so much.

"Why not?" Robert repeated.

"Because...because of her everything's gone wrong here!" She directed a heated look at Anne. "Everything!"

Anne didn't let the impact of the words hitting her show. By now she should be used to them, but she wasn't. She never would be. She kept her gaze on the girl. "I didn't do anything wrong, Mary. I only did what I had to do."

Jamie's hand crept into Anne's under the table. She returned the gentle pressure.

The waitress's face worked, emotion close to the surface. "Because of you my Terry lost his job...and we've had to put off our wedding. But you don't care about that, do you? You don't care about anything...except notoriety. Get your name in the papers, have your face on TV. Have you enjoyed it, Miss Reynolds? Have you enjoyed what you've done to Overton?''

She tried to pull away but Robert's hand was still wrapped about her arm.

''Miss Reynolds hasn't enjoyed any of this. If anything, she's suffered more than anyone else.''

''That I don't believe,'' the girl replied bitterly.

''Ask her, why don't you? Sit down here and *talk* to her.''

''I wouldn't talk to her if she was the last person on earth.''

Robert released the girl's arm with a gesture of disgust. ''Oh, go on. Get away. Take your holier-than-thou attitude and leave.''

The waitress looked momentarily startled.

Robert caught her stare. ''You still here?'' he challenged.

Confusion reigned on the girl's expression. She didn't know what to do. To cover her emotional turmoil, she sniffed and walked stiltedly away.

Anne slid away from the table. ''Come on. Let's leave.''

Jamie, still holding her hand, came with her. For a moment Robert retained his seat. ''I don't think we should.''

''There's a time and place for everything, Robert, and this isn't either.'' She looked around. Everyone had turned back to stare at them. Not one person looked friendly. Her gaze went over them, from one unyielding face to another...until it came to a man sitting on a stool at the far end of the counter. He, too, was staring back at her, but there was something else in his expression besides blank hatred.

Anne had already started for the door when the man stood up and reached in his pocket for change. This he threw on the counter and strode out the door before her.

"Anne, you can't give in like that," Robert was saying as they stepped outside. "People have to learn that you intend to fight, or they'll keep wiping their feet on you."

"It isn't what you think. That place"—she motioned toward the restaurant with her head—"The people in there all worked for Kinkaid Systems. I know them, Robert. And you heard the waitress. Hell would freeze over before..."

A car backed out of a parking spot close by, cutting off Anne's denial. She jumped, not expecting it to come so near. Robert's hand was immediately on her arm, ready to pull her completely clear.

The car stopped and the driver looked at Anne. Surprisingly, after a moment, he nodded. Then he drove away, leaving Anne to stare after him, frowning her puzzlement.

"Who was that?" Robert asked.

"Henry Wynstock. He works—worked—at Kinkaid. He was one of the accountants who came into the print shop that day."

"He doesn't seem to hate your guts as much as the other people do."

"He was right at retirement age. Maybe he wasn't hurt as badly as the rest."

"Could be," Robert agreed. "What we need is a few hundred more like him."

Anne nodded. "What are we going to do about food?"

"Is there a fast-food place in town?"

"One...it's privately owned. Overton isn't big enough for any of the major chains."

"Then we'll go there. I'll place the order and we'll take it back to the motel to eat. Sound okay?"

"I want a hamburger," Jamie cried. "And potato chips!"

Robert smiled at his son. "Not fries?"

Jamie shook his head. "Chips! Chips!"

Robert laughed softly and agreed, "Chips it is."

AN HOUR LATER, while Jamie was down for his nap, Anne and Robert went outside so that they could talk. The motel had provided several benches beneath a grove of oak trees across from the rooms they had rented. Two of the benches were broken but one was serviceable, and it was on that one that they sat.

A slight breeze tousled Anne's hair, causing several strands to tickle her cheek. She put up a hand to brush them away, her eyes ranging over the mountains in the distance, their familiar forms making her heart ache with longing. She had no home. Not in Ohio, not in California. She had no place to call her own and no one to share her isolation with. Robert and Jamie were with her now, but she couldn't expect their continued accompaniment. Not once the problem in Overton was solved.

Robert leaned forward and stared at the ground, not seeing the ants that were industriously going about the business of hunting for and gathering food. He moved his foot, unconsciously presenting a barrier for the tiny insects. Undaunted, they blazed another trail.

He glanced at Anne. Her eyes were focused on the mountains, but he wasn't sure that she was aware of what she was looking at. Her eyes were sad, mirroring her probable thoughts.

He looked away. He remembered the first time he had seen her; he remembered those moments on the beach. And he suddenly found himself wanting to touch her again. Only now there was a difference. This time he knew her. This time he felt that he knew more about himself. Everything else was still uncertain... but he was almost overwhelmed with a consuming need to make contact.

He stirred, quietly clearing his throat.

His movement broke her from her spell. She glanced at him and forced a smile, and he had to physically restrain himself from reaching out to her. He caught hold of the bench on each side of his thighs.

"What are you thinking?" he asked, for something to say.

She glanced at the mountains again. "About life...my life. About how I'm wasting it...how I've always wasted it."

He frowned. "What makes you say that?"

"I've never reached out for it. I've always just sat back and let things happen."

"You didn't when you found the incriminating papers."

She shrugged. "I'm not talking about that."

"What then?"

"The essentials. Like just enjoying today because it's today. Like taking every second and making it count for something. Not just letting it pass to be followed by another and another... until days and years go by and you don't have anything to show for it."

"You sound like you're ninety-five," he teased, but what she said was striking a very familiar chord. It was the same conclusion he had reached himself, not too many weeks before.

"Sometimes I think I am," she replied. "There are so many things I haven't done. I've never been in love—"

The wistful way she said that made his heart give a funny little jolt.

"You find that a failing?" he asked.

She frowned. "It's...an emptiness." She shook her head. "You don't know what I'm talking about. You've been married... you have a child."

Robert knew exactly what she was talking about. It was the same emptiness that he had found in himself. It was the reason he had returned from Asia to locate his son—the dark chasm that had haunted so many of his dreams, and still did when he let down his guard. Jamie had filled a great deal of it—his child meant his life—but there was still a part of himself that he didn't like to look at or even think of often.

"Being married doesn't automatically fill a void," he murmured.

"Having a child does."

"Yes—"

"Why were you away from Jamie for so long?" She caught her breath, suddenly aware of the inappropriateness of her question. He owed her no answers.

He owed her nothing. Just his presence was enough. "I'm sorry. That's really none of my business. I shouldn't have asked."

He shook his head. "Asking is the only way to find out. I was away from him because I was selfish. And immature. I chose my job over fatherhood."

"But you're rectifying that. You're with him now."

Robert laughed shortly. "Sure...I came back when *I* wanted—when Jamie's needed me all his life. I'm surprised he'll have anything to do with me."

"He loves you."

Robert knew it, but he didn't feel that he deserved it. He would pay for the decision he once had made for the rest of his life.

"Are you good at your job?" she asked, changing the subject a degree.

"Pretty good."

Anne recognized understatement when she heard it. "Do you think I've read any of your work?"

"You might have." He named a story from his section of the world that had been widely praised in the States.

"I remember that piece!" She smiled. Their conversation was brightening her.

"I almost got killed getting it. The local authorities didn't appreciate the idea that I was in their town poking around. I had a hell of a time getting out."

"Didn't it win some kind of award?"

He nodded. It had won several awards but he didn't mention them.

"At least you've done something with your life."

"And you haven't?"

"Not really."

"What about bringing those men to justice?"

"I don't count that."

"Why not?"

"Because... because of what happened afterward. I'm not made of stone, you know. I hate what's going on in Overton. Did you see how many people were in that restaurant we left? Maybe eight. I remember going there when it was packed. I hurt a lot of people by what I did. Maybe the people of Overton are correct. Maybe I should have just kept my mouth shut."

Robert turned her toward him, keeping his hands on her shoulders. "Could you have lived with yourself if you'd done that?"

"Can I live with myself that I didn't?" she countered. "I don't have anywhere to go! I don't have a home!"

"We're cleaning up your home."

She waved him off. "That's just a place. I thought it was a home... before we came back. Against all odds, I thought Overton was still my home. But it's not. Not anymore."

"If the people changed their minds..."

"Can you see them doing that?"

Anne jumped up, unable to sit still any longer. She had no idea what the future held for her. Where she would go. What she would do. She had the entire world to choose from... except sometimes such wide choices were an agony unto themselves. Why couldn't her life have been prescribed? Do this, do that... follow the dotted line. A halting sob broke from her lips, which humiliated her. She started to turn away, but Robert's hand shot out to prevent her.

"Anne—"

Anne automatically stiffened. She didn't want his pity. She didn't want anyone's pity. She wanted...she didn't know what she wanted!

Robert slowly got to his feet. He could feel the conflict going on inside her, just as he could feel the conflict growing inside himself. Her skin was smooth...like silk. But he had given his word that he would not cross the barrier they had built between them. He had come with her to Overton to help her, nothing more. He had no ulterior motive. In a bracing way, he had taken pleasure in the fact that he had no selfish motive. For once, he had been thinking of someone else. Putting their needs before his own. And now...

He couldn't stop himself. He stepped closer to her, keeping hold of her hand, consumed with only one thought.

His free hand came out to stroke her cheek. She turned her face upward, her eyes wide, embattled with confusion. For a long moment he merely looked at her, then slowly, he lowered his head, his mouth coming into gentle contact with her own. It was a delicate, butterfly-like kiss. Tentative, questioning, restrained.

Anne drew back, catching a short breath of surprise, both that he had kissed her and how he had kissed her. It held nothing of the practiced smoothness of their initial confrontation on the beach. At that time, she had sensed a hardness in him, a jaded edge. Now, nothing was forced. If anything, uncertainty hovered in the air between them.

His hands moved to her shoulders, his thumbs unconsciously pulsing against the material of her shirt.

Anne swallowed. A field of electrical impulses seemed to move from him to her and back to him again. One part of her mind told her that she should pull away, but she was incapable of such movement. Slowly, she felt herself drawn forward, her eyes remaining on his face, hypnotized.

Røbert's heart was thundering in his chest. He wanted her as he had wanted no woman before. His body had begun to ache. He no longer thought of the past or of the future. Only this moment mattered.

His mouth descended, found its target. For a long few seconds, he was unaware of her response, wrapped totally in his own sensations. Then he felt her arms come out to close around his midsection as her body fitted itself closely against his. Her lips were alive beneath his, moving, responding. She gave a tiny moan when he transferred his mouth to her neck, pushing at her blouse, freeing more silk-soft skin. Her breasts were soft to the touch, warm, inviting.

Anne had closed her eyes. She didn't know when her back had come up against the tree trunk. She shuddered, knowing that she should call a halt to what was happening, but still unable to. Her body was on fire, just as was the body pressed against her.

"Anne—" he breathed. He wanted to lie down with her, to find a place. The motel was behind them . . . a room . . . a bed.

Anne knew what he was asking, what he wanted. She wanted it, too. And suddenly she realized what it was she felt for Robert. Why she had recoiled from the idea of never seeing him again. Why she had come so fully to love his son. She loved him! She knew so little about him . . . but she loved him. Yet because she knew so little about him, she didn't know what he felt for her. Instinctively, she sensed that it was more than mere desire. There had been a great change in him. He was going through an evolution, just as she was. But was this the time to move the liaison to a new, much more unstable base? Would one, the other, or both be unable to find footing?

Anne was trembling as she turned her face away, trembling as he trailed a line of fiery kisses along her neck. She forced herself to push him away. It took several attempts before the procedure was effective.

Robert's breathing was erratic as he drew back to look at her. She had put distance between them, yet she wasn't rejecting him wholly. Not completely. Her eyes were pools of liquid gold as he gazed at her; her own breathing was erratic. She was not trying to deny the depth of what she felt. But she had stopped them. She was not prepared to go any farther.

He moved back a step, respecting her wish even though it was difficult. "I probably should apologize," he murmured huskily.

"There's no need," she breathed. Everything had happened so quickly. She didn't know what to think...how to act. If what had passed between them meant nothing to him, how could she pretend that it had meant nothing to her?

"Then I won't," he murmured. Taking a chance, he ran a finger down her cheek. He felt her tremble of reaction. Some of the uncertainty that had returned to haunt him receded at the sign. "Are you cold?" He gave her the excuse. The sun was setting and a breeze had come up to add its breath of coolness to the land.

She shook her head negatively. She was anything but cold.

He smiled, making her heart skip a beat. "Neither am I."

She couldn't continue to look at him. She was afraid that too much of what she felt—what she had learned—might be in her eyes. She tried to move past him, but he turned with her to walk at her side.

"I didn't plan that," he remarked quietly. "It just . . . happened."

"I didn't think you had."

"But you don't mind?"

If she said she did, she would be a liar. Yet she couldn't just come out and admit . . . "I won't run away this time, if that's what you mean."

His pale gaze moved over her. He wasn't comfortable with the idea that she was associating what had just occurred with what had happened much earlier in their acquaintance. He wasn't proud of what he had done then. "This was different," he urged.

"I know," Anne replied.

He buried his hands in his pockets. He didn't know what else to say. Normally, he fell back on glib words, on practiced assertions. But that was the old Robert. The new Robert was completely at a loss. "Good," he finally said and cursed himself silently for the stupidity of the reply.

Anne's mouth quivered into a smile.

SHE WAS BACK! Randall Elliot could scarcely believe it. But he had heard the report from too many sources. She had been seen in a grocery store, in the restaurant, and she was staying at the old motel on the edge of town—registered under a different name with a man and a young boy. What had she come back to Overton for?

The possible answer to that question struck terror in Randall's heart and he had to hurry to find a seat. He looked about the library... his favorite part of his dream home. He had worked and scraped for years to build it exactly as he wished. And she could take it all away with one word in the right ear. What had she come back for—money?

Randall tried to control his leaping panic. He didn't have that much. And that incompetent fool he had hired to kill her was coming at him for more.

Randall cursed the day he had happened upon Paul and Michael Kinkaid. Of course, if he hadn't gotten involved with them, he would still be dreaming of this house. But had it been worth it? Right now he wasn't so sure.

He wiped the heavy layer of perspiration from his upper lip and felt more wetness cover it again.

He couldn't just sit there and wait. He would have to act...and act himself. He couldn't afford any more foul-ups.

ROBERT INSISTED the next morning that they go into the town proper and walk around for a few hours. The more people who saw Anne the better.

Their first meeting a short time before had been awkward, each thinking of the evening before. They were both unsure, about themselves, about each other. But with Jamie's help—he always seemed to wake up ready to go, his boundless energy not wearing out until he slept—they were able to gloss over those moments and agree on a plan for the day.

Overton consisted of four main streets that radiated away from a town square. The immediate area around the square was the business heart of the small town. Anne's own print shop was in this section. When they came to it, she couldn't help lingering.

Damage had been done here as well. That was what finally had driven her out. She could take the eggs thrown against her front door, the air let out of her car tires, the speeding cars in the middle of the night whose occupants called out vicious vilifications. What had tipped the process had been the damage done to her equipment. With no printing presses, no copiers, no collator, she had lost the heart to continue to fight.

The way some people love art, Anne loved being able to take blank paper and turn it into a thing of beauty. Neat lines, crisp colors. She had taken pride in her work. And until the trial, people had appreciated her work. She had even received orders from towns some distance away.

The day after someone broke into the shop and destroyed the equipment, she left.

Now, as she stood at the window, her hands cupping the sides of her face so that she could see into the gloom, she again experienced the anger and hurt, the personal affront to her pride, that she had suffered that day.

"Is this your place?" Robert asked quietly, at her side.

She nodded, her throat tight with emotion. Everything looked exactly as she had left it: the machines beaten into pieces, ink and supplies strewn everywhere.

"Want to go inside?"

She shook her head no.

Robert peered in the window, copying her stance. When he saw the damage, he understood her reluctance. He stepped back, frowning. "Was it like this before you left?"

Anne cleared her throat. "Yes."

"Did you report it to the police?"

"There wasn't any use. They wouldn't have done anything."

"What about insurance?"

"I have it—but I haven't filed a claim yet." ·

"You should."

She turned on him, letting some of her anger about what had happened bleed onto him. "I should have done a lot of things! But I just didn't. Okay?"

She felt Jamie's small hand creep into hers. She immediately apologized. "I'm sorry. I just . . ."

"Don't worry about it."

Several people looked up as they passed on the sidewalk, their expressions becoming hostile once they recognized her.

Anne's anger wasn't spent. This time she directed it at some of the truly guilty parties. "Good morning, Emily," she challenged. "Nice day, isn't it, Mr. Gowen? Beautiful weather, Billy."

None of them answered. Until, to her surprise, Henry Wynstock, whom she hadn't seen standing in the doorway of the hardware store, called, "Good morning."

All three of them turned to look at him.

Henry Wynstock was a large raw-boned man, whose ancestors had lived on the land for generations. He, though, had struggled to get an education and had been in a position of some power in the accounting department of Kinkaid Systems before it went belly-up. When he stepped out of the doorway, the sun gave a sheen to his balding head.

"So you came back," he said, looking only at Anne.

Anne felt Robert stiffen beside her, ready for anything the man might do.

She nodded. "Yes."

"That takes a lot of courage."

She heard muted voices not too far away. It seemed that they had gathered a curious crowd. That one of them had broken the bond and was talking to her would provide enough grist for the gossip mills for at least two days.

"For what you're doing, too," she acknowledged.

He dismissed her words with a negligent shrug. "It's not that much."

"It's more than anyone else has done."

"Maybe I have more reason than most."

Anne frowned. But before she could make a reply, he had turned away, going back into the hardware store without looking back.

"What did he mean by that?" Robert asked.

"I don't know," Anne answered slowly.

"Could he be the one who...?"

He didn't need to complete the sentence. Anne knew exactly what he was proposing. Once, she would have categorically denied it. Henry Wynstock had always seemed a very gentle man. But time had taught her not to judge people by the persona they showed the world. Time and the people of Overton.

"I don't know that either," she replied.

They continued their promenade—man, woman and child, presenting a brave face, though all the while they were being shunned.

Jamie was particularly quiet. He was too intelligent, too quick, not to notice that he was included in the people's condemnation of Anne. As a result, he held his head high and kept his grasp of her hand—telling the world, even this small part of it, where his loyalties lay.

THE SOLITARY STRANGER in town was noticed by more than one person. Overton wasn't on the tourist track. Its population was fairly steady and consisted of the same group of people. So someone new stood out, especially someone the size and temperament of the man who had stalked into the town's only restaurant that morning and put away a breakfast few could contemplate, let alone eat. After he had finished eating, Jack Minyon sat at the table and contemplated what he would do next. Randall Elliot had called his bluff. He hadn't come across with the money. As far as he could see, that left him with two options: beat the bastard to within an inch of his life and see which he'd rather hold on to: his money or his well-being...or do as he had threatened and go to the newspaper.

Jack used his paper napkin as a nose tissue. At least he didn't think he was going to die of pneumonia any more. His chest was clearing; the cold seemed to be tapering off. Maybe now he could begin to think straight.

He contemplated his options, drinking cup after cup of Overton's best coffee and scowling at the waitress each time she came to ask if he wanted another refill.

Chapter Ten

That afternoon Robert, Anne and Jamie attacked a second room in her house. But this one—the living room—was in far worse condition. They had barely made a dent in the mess when darkness and exhaustion overtook them.

They drove back to the motel in relative silence.

"I don't know if this is doing any good," Anne sighed.

Robert glanced at her. "Give it time. We've only been here a few days."

"But it's all so frustrating!"

"At least no one's tried another accident."

"Maybe they're afraid to, with you so close by."

"Then they've got to be getting pretty frustrated themselves. I think things are going to happen pretty soon."

Anne was so tired even that prospect didn't stir her. "Your nose for news telling you something?"

"It's been itching a lot lately."

She leaned her head back against the rear of the seat and closed her eyes. "I've always heard that meant someone's talking about you."

"Maybe they are—whoever's after you." He took a breath. "Seriously, Anne, I think we'd better brace for something. The feeling's getting stronger each day."

When she made no reply, he took his gaze from the road ahead to glance at her. She had fallen asleep. Her head was tilted to one side; her expression was relaxed.

It might not have been the safest of procedures, but from that point on, Robert took frequent advantage of the time when she wasn't aware of his perusal.

Over the years, he had known many beautiful women. Anne's beauty, though, was all-encompassing. It came from within as well as without, and it made all the others pale in comparison.

When he was forced to direct the car into the motel's front drive, it was almost with a sense of disappointment, because he would lose the unrestricted freedom to look at her.

THE CAR BRAKED SUDDENLY, causing Anne to start awake. She sat up, blinking, trying to adjust her thoughts, trying to understand what had happened.

She looked at Robert, who was staring straight ahead. They had arrived at the motel; she recognized the grounds. What was out of place was the small group of people who were milling about outside their rooms.

He glanced at her, his face grim. "Do you want to go somewhere else for a time? Wait them out?"

Anne contemplated doing just that. Maybe they'd go away. Maybe there would be no further ugliness. But she knew, from experience, that that wouldn't necessarily happen. "No. We'll go on. Unless you'd rather—"

He answered her incomplete question by edging the car forward.

"Why'd you come back?" The rude query was hurled at Anne even before they got out of the car. Someone thumped the car's fender with a fist. More rude comments followed.

Robert opened his door, after murmuring to Anne to stay inside. Without acknowledging the crowd, he pushed his way to the passenger door and opened it. Anne got out, trying to shield Jamie with her body. The boy was confused. He didn't know what was happening.

Someone picked up a rock and threw it. Luckily, it missed. Robert's arm tightened around Anne's shoulders. She felt the anger grow in him.

"All right! That's enough!" he yelled. "That's more than enough. What kind of people are you?"

"We don't need no fancy lawyers...that's the kind we are," someone answered. It was obvious the rumor mill had passed on this item of disinformation.

"If you don't like it, get out!" came another faceless cry.

"Daddy?" Jamie whispered, questioning fear in his voice.

Robert's jaw clenched. "Has any one of you considered the fact that you might be wrong?"

"She's the one who's wrong."

"No!" Robert denied. "You are! Look what you're doing here. You're a mob...and you're frightening a child."

"We can't help it if she brought her bastard along with her this time."

Robert's arm dropped away from Anne's shoulders. He stalked toward the man who had spoken. Anne didn't know the man's name, but she recognized his face. She had often seen him around town before everything went wrong. He had drifted from one low-paying job to another.

"Would you like to repeat that?" Robert taunted softly. He was practically nose to nose with the man.

The man started to repeat his words, then thought better of the idea when he noticed that the rest of the crowd had backed away.

"Right," Robert clipped. He could sense the turn of the crowd's purpose. The bluster was beginning to disappear. Soon they, too, would disappear. But before they did, he turned to narrow his gaze on each of them. "Miss Reynolds is owed an apology. By each of you. By everyone in this town. What you did to her—what you're doing—is unforgivable. Turn what she did around: if it had happened to you...if you had found the papers that she did...how would you have acted? Those men were selling government secrets! Your government's secrets! For profit. For their profit. If you want to be angry...be angry at them. They're the ones who gambled with your town's well-being. Don't tell me they were thinking of Overton when they decided to do what they did. They were thinking only of themselves. And Overton paid the price. Miss Reynolds, here, is as much a victim as you are."

"But she got herself on TV," someone protested.

Robert laughed harshly. "What happened was news. She didn't ask for it. She only did what she felt she had to do. Did anyone stop to ask if she was enjoying it? I can guarantee she wasn't. Who in their right mind would want to suffer what she has?"

Many of the people began to shuffle uneasily. Some were hearing a point of view that they hadn't thought of before. Others merely wanted to get away; what was happening was no longer exciting.

"Think about it," Robert advised. "And don't try this again. Frightening a child isn't something to be proud of."

He turned away to walk back to Anne. Anne held her head proudly. She felt the people looking at her, at them, and she was not going to ruin the effect of Robert's words by appearing downcast.

The crowd dispersed as they walked through it. Murmurings could be heard, but no one tried to impede their way, or to hurt them in any other manner. By the time they got to the twin doors to their rooms, the entire area was deserted. The people had faded into the night, leaving behind only a quiet malaise.

UPON ENTERING HER ROOM, Anne released a shaky breath. Jamie was clinging to her leg, one arm wrapped tightly about her jeans. Robert stood at the door a moment before closing it and locking it.

"I think that's the last we'll hear from them."

"I hope so." Anne was not as optimistic as he was. At this point, nothing the people of Overton did would surprise her.

Robert glanced at his son. He saw the fear that was still haunting his expression. To cheer him, he proposed, "Why don't we give your mother a call? Would you like that, sport?"

Jamie blinked and loosened his hold. "Right now?" he asked.

"Sure, why not?"

The boy slid a glance at Anne and when she nodded encouragement, he moved to his father's side. "'Kay," he agreed, but not with as much enthusiasm as he might have earlier.

Anne caught at her bottom lip. All of this was having a bad effect on Jamie. He should never have come. Robert was looking at her over his son's head. His eyes told her that he was thinking the same thing, then he said, completing the unspoken thought, "There was no other choice."

Father and son went into their room to make the call and Anne stretched out on the bed, her muscles aching from the exertions of the day. She turned her head toward the door. It took a moment before she saw the envelope on the floor. In the upset over getting into the room, no one had noticed it lying there. She went to retrieve it. There was no name on the front and the back flap was unsealed.

Anne looked at it curiously before pulling the message inside into view.

We have something to talk about. Come to the gazebo at 12:30 tonight. Don't bring anyone with you.

The letter was unsigned. Anne read it again. Then she crumpled it and stuffed it in her pocket as she heard Robert reenter the room.

He frowned when she jerked around. Her face looked odd...pale. He concluded that she was still suffering from what had happened.

"At least they didn't have a rope," he teased wryly.

"They probably could have found one easily enough." She was wholly aware of the letter in her pocket, of what it said. She was torn between telling Robert and not telling him.

He didn't hesitate to come closer. When he put his arms around her and drew her close, Anne didn't protest. She needed his warmth, the reassurance of his heartbeat.

"Were you frightened?" he whispered. The top of her hair tickled his chin, the softness of her body intoxicated him. But he held himself in check. She had been through too much recently.

She lifted her head to look at him. "A little."

"I was, too—for you."

Anne pushed away. Turning, she fell to the pretext of combing her hair. She couldn't face what she had discovered last night at this moment. She couldn't do as she wished and cling to him as Jamie had clung to her earlier.

"I'm tired, Robert. Would you mind—?"

His face stiffened slightly. Her withdrawal had been more than physical. He didn't understand. Didn't she approve of what he had done when he faced down the crowd? Or was it the easy way he had come to embrace her?

"Of course. I'm tired, too." He paused. "Is anything wrong?"

Anne shook her head. "No...nothing."

He was still frowning as he said good night and closed the door between their two rooms.

ANNE KNEW THE GAMBLE she was taking. She knew Robert would be angry if he found out. But this was something she had to do. She couldn't involve him anymore. He might get hurt.

She smoothed the note out on the bed and read it once again. It was stark, clear and to the point: come and come alone. Was it from the person who wanted to have her killed? If she went, would she be walking into a trap?

But if she didn't go, would it ever end? This was what they had wanted to happen when they came back to Overton. They wanted the killer to tip his hand, to expose himself. Yet how could she protect herself? She had no weapon, no gun...and even if she did, she didn't know how to use one.

She had only one thing: her intellect. She would go, but she would go on her own terms.

THE SQUARE WAS HAUNTED by sounds from the past: Spanish dons, early American settlers, those with the fever for gold. Overton had once been a stagecoach stop. Today, children played in the branches of its trees while their mothers and fathers shopped. Overton had not lived up to the promise of its beginning. It had not lived up to the promise of its immediate past. At night, though, echoes blended and failed hopes dimmed to become the ghosts of a future day.

Anne glided from tree to tree, making no sound. She was early, but that was part of her plan.

Her heart thumped thickly in her chest as the gazebo came into closer view. Was he already there? Could he have the same plan as she? And why did she think that whoever it was was a he? It could be anyone.

Anne came closer, still hiding in the dark night. Normally there was light filtering into the square from the lamps scattered along the nearby streets. But tonight, for some reason, the closest lights were out of order, and only the moon and stars spilled muted radiance onto the grounds. Anne wasn't sure if that was a good sign or not. It helped her in her determination not to be easily seen, but it also helped her adversary in just the same manner.

She watched the gazebo for several long seconds before determining that it was vacant. Taking a deep breath, she ran across the clearing and buried herself behind a concealing cluster of bushes that grew at the gazebo's side. There she would wait until 12:30.

RANDALL ELLIOT WALKED quickly away from his home, keeping to the darker shadows along the sidewalk. He hadn't brought his car. He didn't want any trouble from whichever deputy sheriff was on duty that night. He didn't want to have to answer any questions.

Nervously, he wiped his mouth. His entire body felt wired. It wasn't a pleasant experience. He wondered if she would come...if she would come alone. He didn't want to have to deal with the man she was with. Rumor had it that he was a lawyer. That was exactly what he didn't need.

The square loomed ahead, satisfactorily dark. It paid to have access to the public works department. Tomorrow, someone would catch hell for this evening's work, but no one would ever connect the occurrence with himself.

He had wanted the square to be fairly dark and it was darker than he hoped. Again, he hadn't wanted a deputy sheriff to blunder into his meeting with Anne Reynolds. What they had to say to each other was private. He only hoped she would see reason.

His stomach flipped at the possibility that she wouldn't.

WHEN SHE HAD BEEN in position for over an hour, Anne finally heard a noise. She became perfectly still, her head low, her body crouched close to the ground. But she was able to peek out through the leaves and see that someone was approaching. He was moving almost as stealthily as she had earlier—only he was trailing along the sidewalk, staying close to the tree cover there. She pulled her face back into the darkness, not wanting to give herself away.

She heard the footsteps get closer and then take the short series of steps that led into the gazebo.

The man stopped. It was a man, she was sure, because of the way he walked and the heaviness of his footsteps on the wooden flooring. She heard him light a cigarette, curse softly and then stamp it out.

Anne stayed quiet. She decided to make him wait.

Some moments later, after hearing another soft curse, she swallowed, knowing that the time had come. With absolute quietness, she stood up. She could see him standing a little way from her, several feet higher than she was, leaning on the banister, looking out at the street.

"You wanted to see me?" Her voice, quiet though it was, shattered the still air.

The man whirled around as she stepped out of the bushes. He had nothing in his hands; she had made sure of that.

In the filtered light, she recognized him. Anyone who had lived in Overton for any time would.

Randall Elliot stared at her as if she were an apparition, his hands clenching on the banister to steady his suddenly weakened frame. How much did she know? Did she know that he had tried to have her killed?

"Miss Reynolds," he managed.

Anne gazed at him warily. "Why did you ask me here, Mr. Elliot?"

Randall took a deep breath. "Why don't you come up here where we can talk easier?" he suggested.

"No," Anne replied. "You didn't answer my question."

He closed the distance that separated them along the gazebo. When he was directly across from her, he said, "It would be easier to do business if we could see each other."

"You chose the meeting place."

He leaned forward. He always dressed neatly, and a rendezvous of this sort was no exception. His short dark hair was combed into place, and he wore a suit that fitted his athletic form perfectly. Randall Elliot had been the pride of Overton for most of his life. The citizens had lived in his reflected glory as he played outstanding football from high school through college. An injury in his senior year gave him the excuse not to try the greater punishment of the professional ranks, but he never confided to anyone his relief. He traded on his past glories, as many men did.

He made himself smile. "Just what is it you want from me, Miss Reynolds?"

"I don't want anything from you, Mr. Elliot."

"Oh, come now. Everyone wants something. Particularly people in your position."

Anne frowned. "What position is that?"

Randall Elliot stiffened, his teeth no longer gleaming in the starlight. "Don't play stupid with me. I don't have time for it. Just tell me what you want and I'll see what I can do about it. Only I'm warning you . . . I don't have all that much."

"Did you try to have me killed, Mr. Elliot?" Anne asked softly.

He took her question like an arrow in the heart. She heard the tiny gasp he gave. "All right!" he said hoarsely. "All right! I can get more. But it has to be only once, do you hear me? Only once!"

"I don't know what you're talking about," Anne said. She was beginning to form an idea but nothing was certain yet. It was exactly as Robert had said: he was afraid of her. But why?

"I'm sure you don't," he returned nastily. "You don't think I'm stupid, do you? I know one of those papers had my name on it. And I know you kept it from the authorities for a reason. What was your reason . . . if it wasn't to get money out of me?"

Everything fell into place. It all revolved around the trial! Randall Elliot had been involved with the Kinkaids! Only no one had known. He certainly hadn't been mentioned in the papers that had been left at her print shop.

He was afraid of her...of what she might know...of what she might do with that knowledge. Reputation meant everything to a man like Randall Elliot. If he thought that she held the key to his destruction, he would try to get rid of the key...if not in one way, then in another.

A shudder passed over her body. She was standing face to face with the man who wanted her dead. Who probably still wanted her dead but was willing to deal with her, if he had to.

"There were no papers with your name on them," she said.

"I don't believe you."

Anne shrugged. How was she going to get out of this?

"How much do you want? Five thousand, ten?"

"I don't want your money, Mr. Elliot."

"You don't—" he repeated incredulously, and then stopped. "What else is it then?" he demanded, becoming angry.

"I had no idea you were involved with the Kinkaids. Not until you told me just now."

"You..." he stammered.

"There's no proof."

"I don't believe you!" he shouted, then immediately hushed his tone to keep from drawing the attention of anyone who might be out in the quiet night. "If you think—" he puffed "—that I'm going to just sit still while you... I won't do it, you know. I won't sit still. If I can't get through to you one way, I'll get through to you in another. I'll make you regret not telling me the truth. I won't live with this hanging over my head!''

Anne took a step back. In his agitation, he was very different from the man she had known casually, because of his position in the town. Looking at him now, hearing him, she could see that he was beginning to break emotionally.

She took another step away before turning to run into the protection of the trees. Her heart was racing, her breath was short—and not merely from her sprint to safety. She believed what he was saying. She believed that he would do whatever he could to harm her... and all because of the mistaken notion that she was hiding something that would implicate him. Something she didn't have. Something that, if she had it, she would happily give him in order to get her life back to normal again.

''You'll regret it!'' his voice followed her. Then it was immediately hushed, and she ran all the faster back along the streets that led to the motel.

ANNE SLIPPED BENEATH THE SHEETS, her body trembling with shock and dread. What would he do next? She brought her hand up to her mouth and bit on her finger to keep from crying out. Should she wake Robert... tell him what she had done, what she had discovered?

Nothing had changed, except that she now had a face and a name.

Nothing had changed at all. She was still helpless in the face of an insurmountable problem.

She didn't have any paper and Randall Elliot didn't believe her.

He was almost mad with fear.

What would he do next?

Chapter Eleven

Anne was not the only person distracted the next morning as she, Robert and Jamie sat around the small table in her room picking at the meager breakfast Robert had procured from a nearby grocery store.

Jamie poked at his muffin, crumbling it rather than eating it; Robert was eating his, but absently, not tasting it. Anne's stomach was in too much turmoil to even contemplate food. She focused her gaze on the television set where someone was reading the news, but she wasn't listening.

Should she tell Robert? The question was circling in her mind. One part of her wanted to...but her more realistic self told her that when he learned who the person was, he would immediately want to confront him. And Anne was afraid that Randall Elliot, in his crazed state, might do him serious harm.

She didn't want that. She didn't want Robert to be hurt. When you love someone, you desire only the best for them...and that was what she wanted for Robert, and for Jamie. And Jamie needed his father.

Yet if she didn't tell him, how would he react if he ever learned the truth? And if he didn't learn it, how much longer would he insist that they stay here?

He had taken a leave of absence from his job, originally to be with Jamie. But that couldn't last forever.

Yet if she told him . . . The thoughts continued to circle.

Robert dropped the last bite of his muffin back to his plate. He glanced at Anne. She seemed absorbed in what the newscaster on television was saying. He sighed.

He didn't know what to do. Last night, after he had left Anne, Karen had told him that she wanted Jamie to come back. She was feeling lousy and feeling sorry for herself. And she said that she didn't care what Bryce wanted anymore . . . she wanted Jamie back.

But how could he bring him back now? He hadn't been kidding when he told Anne that he sensed the affair in Overton would soon be over. That something was about to break. He felt it in his bones, which meant that he couldn't go racing off to deliver the boy to Karen. Anne needed him. If anything happened to her while he was gone, he would never forgive himself.

Yet Jamie was beginning to suffer the effects of the hostility here. Last night he had been shaken. He had even cried out several times in his sleep.

Robert rubbed his forehead. He seemed to jump from one mistake to another in his handling of his son. Whichever way he stepped seemed fraught with problems. If he took Jamie back to Karen, would Bryce make his life even more difficult? The tensions between Karen and her husband seemed to have multiplied as the end of her pregnancy drew near.

Then there was the question of Jamie's loyalty to Anne. Would the child want to leave?

He glanced at his son who was unusually quiet that morning.

"Don't play with your food, Jamie," he directed softly.

Jamie looked up, startled. Then he gave a shadow of his old grin and immediately stuffed several pieces of muffin into his mouth.

Robert smiled slightly. Jamie knew that his mother wanted him to come back. Karen had talked with the boy until he was almost asleep sitting up. That was when he had taken the line and she had berated him for everything she could think of, along with berating her present husband for being a selfish fool, before she broke into tears and hung up.

That was another reason Robert was hesitant about what to do with the boy. Karen was in no state to take proper care of him.

But then, at the moment, was he?

He shifted position in his chair, gaining Anne's attention. Oddly, he noticed that her body tensed before she looked quickly away.

Last night he had sensed something in her behavior. Today, it was still there.

"Did you sleep well last night?" he asked politely.

"I slept all right," she replied, but her voice was tight.

He frowned. Something was wrong.

"Then what—?" he started to ask when she interrupted.

"Just...leave it alone, okay? I'm fine, you're fine, Jamie's fine. That's all that matters."

Jamie had finished his muffin and was sitting there, wide-eyed, watching the two adults.

Robert glanced at him and held his tongue. There definitely was more to it than that, but he wouldn't press her while the boy was listening so intently.

Anne felt the tension in her body. She hadn't meant to snap at him. She loved him! But it was because of that love that she had to fight to keep in control.

THEY DIDN'T WORK as late at the house as they had the previous day. There had been no banter, no laughter to pass the time, and strain lay over each of them like a blanket.

When they arrived back at the motel it was still light, but Anne went directly to her room to lie down. She needed time to be alone...to think.

Robert sat on the bedcover, his back against the drably colored wall. Jamie stretched out on the opposite bed and soon fell into a deep sleep.

Robert swiveled his gaze to his son and watched him as he breathed, somehow reassured by that gentle process. A half hour later, he became sleepy himself.

JAMIE ROUSED FROM SLEEP and sat up to rub his eyes. The room was quiet. He looked around, his mind momentarily filling with panic until he saw his father asleep on the other bed.

Jamie slung his feet from the bed and dropped them to the floor. He leaned over his father. Yep, he was asleep all right.

He sighed. He didn't like living in this place. There wasn't enough room. Not even when Anne's door was open.

He stole over to that door and carefully opened it. She was in bed, too. Not moving. He giggled softly. He was the only one awake!

Then a frown settled on his clear brow. They didn't know he knew, but he did. They were here to find the bad man who had tried to run them off the road...who had tried to hurt Anne. He thought of the people from the night before—the way they had looked, the way they had acted. He had been frightened.

He closed the door and went back to sit on the end of the bed, kicking the back of his heels against the spread.

If they came again, he'd show 'em. He'd pick up a rock . . . just like one of them had. And he'd . . . Jamie twisted his shoulders. His mother wouldn't like that. Neither would his father. He'd get into trouble.

Thinking of his mother made Jamie sad. She had cried when she talked to him. She said Bryce was being mean. That they weren't going to pay any attention to him . . . that she wanted him to come back.

Jamie jumped from the bed. He wanted to help Anne, but he also wanted to be with his mother.

He found the tiny metal car that was one of his favorite toys and began to run it along the chest of drawers that rested against one wall. The car traveled from chest of drawers to floor to the door leading outside.

The car wanted to go outside and play. So did he.

Jamie glanced at his father. He was still sleeping.

Jamie remembered the motel's swimming pool and he quickly tore off his jeans and shirt and slipped into his swim trunks.

Then, his car at the ready, Jamie quietly opened the door and closed it.

The sidewalk made a perfect freeway for his car.

ROBERT ROLLED OVER with a groan. He hadn't meant to sleep. He had just been sitting there, thinking, when— He suddenly sat upright, looking at the empty bed at his side.

"Jamie?" he questioned.

There was no answer.

"Jamie," he called again, making his voice stronger. He got to his feet and went to the bathroom to look inside. He thought that possibly the boy was in there.

The room was empty.

Icy fear shot through Robert's body. He gripped the molding at the side of the door to steady himself. Jamie was gone!

Then he remembered that the boy might have gone to be with Anne.

Quick steps took him to her door. He opened it without notice.

Anne sat up, groggily trying to make her eyes focus. Robert was in the doorway, his face tight, his expression intense.

"Is Jamie in here with you?" he asked, afraid that he already knew the answer.

Anne slid to her feet, unconsciously running a hand through her hair. "No—" She looked helplessly around. "I don't think so."

"Check in the bathroom," he ordered.

She did as he directed while he swept the outside door open. She was coming back into the room when he returned, a pained look marking his features.

"He's not there," she said.

Robert didn't reply. He jerked open the door again and she heard the pounding of his feet as he called the boy's name.

She didn't bother to slip on her shoes. Anxiety clutched at her heart. What had happened while she slept? Where could the boy be? She followed Robert out the door, running just as he did.

Her voice joined with his as they covered the distance around the motel. They checked the pool, the parking lot, the lobby. The boy was nowhere to be found.

Robert's breathing was jagged when he finally stopped running. Anne halted at his side, her breathing just as unsteady.

"Where could he be?" she panted.

Robert shook his head.

"Maybe he's come back to the room," she suggested.

Robert closed his eyes then hurried away. With each step that she took, Anne prayed that she would be right.

She wasn't. The rooms were still empty.

Robert moaned as they stood in his vacant room. Anne's heart went out to him. She put her hand on his shoulder. His muscles quivered beneath her fingers.

"Should we try the other rooms?" she asked, trying to think of something to be of help.

"There's only one other person besides us at the motel." He had kept careful watch of their surroundings.

"Then we'll check with him."

Robert nodded. For a moment his eyes were dull. Before he had gotten his post in South Asia, he had done his share of reporting in the States. He had even covered one young child's disappearance from the beginning to the end... and the outcome hadn't been good. *Where was he? Where could he have gone?* The questions ricocheted in his mind like bullets.

"What room is he in?" Anne asked. She hadn't been as observant as Robert.

"One at the other end of the court."

They hurried out the door, Anne in the lead this time.

A man in scruffy clothes answered their impatient knock.

"Yeah?" he asked, not pleased at having been disturbed by people as obviously overwrought as these.

Anne rushed into speech before Robert. "Have you seen a little boy... blond, six years old?"

"Haven't seen him," the man answered and tried to close the door.

Robert's hand shot out to prevent it. "We'd like a little more information."

"You asked if I saw him and I gave you an answer. What more do you want?"

"To look around your room," Robert said without hesitation.

"To—" the man hissed. He drew himself up to his full height, which was formidable. "Are you trying to say that I took him?" he demanded.

Robert sighed. "Look. My little boy's missing. We're just trying to cover all bases before we call the police."

His last words worked like a magic incantation. The door immediately swung open. "Look all you want," the man invited. "He ain't here."

What the man said was true. Robert stepped outside and thanked him for his trouble, then he rubbed a weary hand against the muscles of his neck.

Anne asked, "What do we do now?"

"Talk to the police?" he answered with a question.

She bit her bottom lip. "They're not going to be too friendly."

"I don't give a damn how friendly they are. They can help us find Jamie."

As Anne had warned, the uniformed man sitting in Overton's sheriff's office was not all that anxious to stir himself to help.

"Kids go missing all the time," he said, lying back in his chair with his feet propped on his desk.

"This kid wouldn't do that," Robert returned, angry at the man's attitude.

The man shrugged. "Never know," he said. His eyes were on Anne, narrowed, steady.

"Please, Martin," she requested. "Help us."

The chair squeaked as he sat up. "Like you helped us, Miss Reynolds?"

"I've had about all of that I want to hear," Robert snarled, lunging forward.

Martin didn't back down. The two men faced each other. "Is that a threat?" the lawman inquired silkily.

Robert had never wanted to hit someone as much as he wanted to hit this man. But Jamie was missing...he needed his help.

"This isn't a usual case," he said tightly. "You, more than most, should know that. I don't know if someone in this town has gone nuts and wants to hurt the child in order to hurt Anne and me...or what. But something's happened and I want action taken."

"Maybe you should have thought about your son's safety before you brought him here."

"We didn't have a choice!" Robert shouted.

The deputy stood up. "I think you'd better get out of my office."

"You're not going to help?" Robert demanded, his hands clenching into fists.

The man didn't answer.

Robert ground his teeth, his mind scattering on possibilities. He would do whatever it took. He had to find Jamie. "If you don't help," he stated, "I'll have the media all over this place. They'll look and they'll probe. And I promise you they'll find something. Newspeople always do when they look hard enough. At the very least it will be embarrassing...if not criminal." He glanced at Anne. "Did you know that someone's been trying to kill her? How do we know how far it goes? If anything happens to her...or to my son..."

"That's enough! Either get out or I'll put you in jail for creating a disturbance." He ground out the words but something Robert said had disturbed him. He wasn't quite as arrogant as he was before.

"What will you do about my son?" Robert demanded, not backing down.

The man twirled his chair around so that he could sit in it again. "I'll keep a look out. Ask a few people."

"That's not good enough!"

"It's all I'm willing to do. Now get out!"

Robert pulled a picture from his wallet. "Here," he said. "This is what he looks like."

The man took the picture and flipped it onto his desk. Then he turned away from them, pretending to bury himself in paperwork.

ANNE AND ROBERT returned to the motel. As the late evening dusk increased, so did their worry.

"What do you think . . . ?" Anne started to ask and then stopped herself.

Robert shook his head. "We'll look around here another time and then I'm going out to cruise around. Overton's not that big."

"Do you think he'd just go off without telling you?"

"You mean run away?"

Anne thought for a moment and shook her head. No, Jamie was not that kind of child. He was sensitive, thoughtful.

She took a trembling breath. "This is all my fault."

Robert drew her into his arms and held her there. Both of them needed the comfort of the other.

"I should never have let you come," she whispered into his chest. "This was my fight, not yours."

"I made it my fight."

"I still don't understand—"

"Love makes you do crazy things sometimes."

Anne stiffened. She pulled back to look at him. "What?"

"You heard me."

"But—"

He shook his head and pulled her back against him. "Just don't ask questions now. We'll talk about it later . . . after we find Jamie."

Anne wanted to cry, but she didn't let herself. She had to be strong—for Robert, for herself and for Jamie.

ANNE WAITED AT THE MOTEL while Robert drove the streets, talking to people as he went, forcing them to give an answer. No one had seen anything, of course. Still, he alerted them to the fact that the boy was missing.

Henry Wynstock was standing outside the drugstore waiting for a prescription to be filled when he happened to notice Robert driving slowly by, talking to everyone that he saw. He pushed away from the doorway.

Robert recognized him immediately.

"What's up, son?" Henry drawled.

"My little boy . . ." Robert answered. "He's disappeared."

Henry Wynstock frowned. "Is there anything I can do?"

Robert still didn't know whether the man was a friend or a foe with a motive, but he decided to trust Anne's instincts about him. "You can help me talk to people. They don't want to listen. I figure if we get everyone in town to look for him . . ."

"People here have long memories."

"Do you think what Anne did was wrong?" Robert demanded.

"Nope."

"Then why does everyone else?"

Henry shifted position. "Not everyone does. But enough do that count."

Robert muttered a curse.

"I've seen your boy. Everyone has. We'll all start to look," the older man stated.

Robert snarled, "But not the people who count."

Henry tilted his head. "Not even those people are bad people. They're just hurt and don't know where to plant their stinger."

"I would have thought it was obvious."

"You'd be surprised how un-obvious things can get sometimes. Don't worry. We'll find your boy."

ANNE PACED THE SMALL ROOMS, jumping at imagined noises, berating herself for having gotten them involved. She could have denied everything and kept to herself as she had originally planned. But then she wouldn't have gotten to know either of them. And she wouldn't have opened herself up to love.

Loving sometimes hurt...hurt badly. Was that why her father made no move to love her? Showed her no affection? Had he been afraid to love?

She paced across the room again. She'd never know. That was one mystery in life that was closed. Only her father knew the answer and he was gone. But it helped to center on a speculation.

Only it didn't help Jamie. And he was the one in need of help right now. Her imagination started to run away with her again. She thought of all the awful things that could happen to a child.

She moved to the door to look outside. It was so dark. Where could he be?

Then an echo of a threat sounded in her mind. Randall Elliot had told her she'd regret not cooperating with him. Not letting him pay her off, even though she had nothing to give him in return. Could Randall Elliot be behind what had happened to Jamie? The idea terrified her.

Her breath caught in her throat as the telephone in the room behind her rang. She turned to stumble toward it.

"Yes— Hello?"

"Is this room E-3?"

"Yes," she answered breathlessly. Maybe it was someone about Jamie.

"Is Robert Singleton there?"

"Not now. Can I help? Have you any information on..."

Her words were cut off. "This is Bryce Jennings. Karen's husband. I—I just wanted to tell him that Karen died this morning. She was having a difficult delivery and just...died. The baby didn't make it either."

Anne's knees suddenly collapsed. She sank onto the side of the bed. "I'm sorry." She tried to make her brain function. "Is—is there anything we can do?"

Bryce Jennings laughed shortly. It was not amused laughter. He sounded strained. "Her funeral is in three days. He can come to that if he wants." Then the line was disconnected.

Anne sat staring at the wall for a long time, the telephone still in her hand. Jamie's mother had died.

Slowly she replaced the handset on the receiver. There was no way that she could tell Robert... not now. She didn't know where he was. And how would he react? Especially with Jamie missing.

The tears Anne had been fighting to hold back suddenly rushed into her eyes.

One thing followed another. How much more would they all have to endure?

ROBERT WAS BONE-WEARY as he walked to the motel room. On the drive back, he had shut his mind to everything but the certainty that they would find Jamie unharmed. He tried not to think about how frightened the boy would be, or how dark the night was, or how dangerous some monsters who termed themselves human could be.

When he let himself into his room, Anne rushed in from the room opposite. She froze in the doorway. She didn't have to ask; she could see disappointment and worry etched in every line of his face. For a moment she remained still. Then, hurling herself forward, she rushed into his arms—crying, murmuring assurances, silently asking assurance for herself.

Robert crushed her to him, cradling her head against his chest, then lifted it so that he might kiss her.

The kiss was long but not passionate. It was more each giving nurture to the other.

She murmured his name, the aching sound catching fire in his soul as it was answered in like misery.

Anne pushed away, unwilling to give up his nearness, but knowing that she had to. She wiped the tears from her cheeks with her fingertips, but found that her action did little good as more came to take the place of the others.

Robert reached into his pocket for a handkerchief. She sniffed her thanks as she tried to gain control.

"Had anyone seen him?" she asked, her voice a husky whisper.

"No."

"Would they talk to you?"

"Not really. Henry Wynstock did. He said he'd get some people together to help."

"I told you he was a good man."

Robert reserved judgment.

Anne took a deep breath. "While you were out . . . you had a call."

His head lifted sharply.

"Not—not about Jamie." She hurried to correct the impression. "It—it was Bryce Jennings. He . . ." She couldn't make the words come. She didn't want to add to his distress, but there was no way that she could hide the information. "Karen died trying to deliver their baby. It . . . happened this morning."

Robert stood perfectly still, his face draining of what little color that it had. "Karen died?" he asked dully.

Anne nodded. "The baby died, too."

Robert sat down on the bed and Anne hurried to his side. She placed an arm about his shoulders. They were hunched, as a man's shoulders might be who had received one too many burdens.

"He said the funeral would be in three days . . . that you could come if you wanted to." She knew the last sounded forced, possibly even callow. But that had been part of the message, and she didn't want Robert to wonder about it later.

He barely noticed. He sat absolutely still while Anne remained at his side.

Finally, he shook himself free of his daze. "Was that all he said?"

"Yes."

Robert gave a deep sigh.

"Did you still love her?" she asked softly. Maybe it would help him to talk.

"No. I never really did. But—"

"But you had a bond: Jamie."

Again he nodded. "I can't believe—"

Anne knew that she would have to hurt him again. But she had to tell him now. It couldn't wait any longer—not if Randall Elliot was behind Jamie's disappearance.

"Robert. There's something else . . ." she began. "I know who did it. I know who's been trying to have me killed."

Robert's head came up, his gaze immediately centering on her.

Anne wanted to turn away. Yet she made herself continue to look at him.

"There was a note. Last night. I found it after we came inside. It— I— After everyone was asleep I went to meet the man who wrote it."

Robert drew a quick breath, as if what she said had shocked him.

She rushed on. "I was careful. I was very careful. I didn't get close to him. He—he thinks I know something about him that I don't...at least, I didn't...not until after he told me. He was involved with the Kinkaids. He thought he was mentioned in one of the papers I found and that I had kept his name out of it in order to... He offered me money not to tell. When I told him that I knew nothing, he threatened me. He told me that I'd be sorry..." Her breath caught. "I'm afraid he might have Jamie."

Robert remained perfectly still, trying to process what she had told him. His mind didn't seem to want to work. First, Jamie's disappearance, then Karen's death...now Anne was telling him that she had put herself in such danger...

He moved, feeling sluggish, feeling lost. His hands came out to grip her arms. Somehow, she didn't feel real to him. And yet she was the only reality that he had to grasp onto at that moment.

"You could have been killed," he said at last, his words husky even to his own ears.

His grip was painful, but Anne knew that he had no awareness of that fact. She suffered the hurt without comment.

"You little fool," he murmured, his hands working against her skin.

Anne's bottom lip began to tremble. "I wanted to tell you. I wanted to tell you right away, but I..."

"Don't ever do anything like that again. Not ever again."

"Do you think he might have Jamie?" she whispered.

Robert put a finger to her lip to keep it from quivering. "Who is it? Who's the man?"

"His name's Randall Elliot. He works in the town government. He's one of the powers here. One of the movers and shakers. He—" She breathed deeply. "I'm not sure how stable he is anymore. He's afraid, just as you said. So he might be capable of doing anything. And if he has Jamie..."

"What makes you think he might have him?"

Anne wiped away a silent tear. She shrugged. "I don't know...just something...just something he said."

Robert's mind worked on the problem. It was the only solution he could see. Jamie wouldn't have just walked away. He had to have been taken. Only by whom? Anne's nemesis was the only person with cause. And if he was as dangerous as she thought him to be...

Robert reached for the telephone, trying to still the new dimension in terror that had taken hold of his heart. "Maybe the sheriff's office will listen now," he said as he began to dial. Then he added grimly, "They'd better listen."

JAMIE SAT QUIETLY in one corner of the basement, his eyes keeping track of the man who had jerked him off his feet as he played by the side of the pool. He had yelled, but no one had heard him and the man had continued to walk until they reached a car, where he threw him inside and drove away.

The man was tall, almost as tall as his father. And he walked like he had ants crawling all over his body.

He couldn't seem to stand still. And he was muttering things to himself, things Jamie didn't understand.

"Please," Jamie called. "Could I have a drink of water? Please, mister?"

The man looked at him blankly, almost as if he didn't want to see that he was there. Then he continued his pacing and his muttering and Jamie wondered when he was going to let him go.

JACK MINYON TRIED to make himself invisible in his car, which was nearly impossible for a man of his bulk to do. He had been sitting there for an hour, waiting for something to happen, waiting for the right moment to make something happen.

Randall Elliot thought he had called his bluff. Well, he would just have to eat that thought. Because, he, Jack Minyon, would not be cheated out of what was due him. One way or another the man would pay.

Jack smiled to himself. His grandmother would be proud. He had screwed up once, but he wouldn't let it happen again.

He had almost had a heart attack when Anne Reynolds and that man she had in tow showed up on his doorstep looking for the boy. But she hadn't recognized him. She was too upset.

It hadn't taken Jack long to put two and two together. And if he had miscalculated and the youngster had merely gotten lost or run away, he would still take his displeasure out on Randall Elliot... just for the fun of it. If he had the boy, though, what better opportunity to throw a monkey wrench into the works. It would be a touch of poetic justice.

He had driven immediately to Elliot's address, and had taken up a position outside, in the car, to watch and wait. He didn't think much of Elliot's brain-power; but he guessed that Elliot had brought the boy to his home and would soon realize the error of that reasoning and rush out to hide him somewhere else. His gamble had paid off. Within half an hour, Elliot's car had zoomed out of his driveway, and Jack had seen the top of a pale blond head pop up in the passenger seat before it was roughly pushed back down.

He smiled. The idiot. Just what good did he think kidnapping the child would do?

Retaining that smile, he slowly eased himself from the car. He was just outside the downtown section of the little hick town. Not too far from some sort of storage facility. Slowly, he began to walk toward the place where Randall Elliot had parked his car.

UNBELIEVABLY, THE DEPUTY listened to what Robert and Anne had to say during the telephone call. Anne told him everything about Randall Elliot, leaving nothing out. This time, he sounded interested. He told them to sit tight; that he would have a little talk with Randall.

An hour passed, then another hour.

Robert could barely sit still. He went outside several times to pace in the cold night air, smoking the cigarettes he had at one time denied himself.

Anne fared little better. If only they knew what was happening!

Robert had settled into a chair and Anne was sitting across from him when a knock on the door caused them both to jump.

Robert stood up to answer it. Anne followed closely behind him.

A large man was standing outside—a neatly dressed man with a thick neck and burly shoulders.

"You have to promise not to ask any questions," he began. "I think I found something you've lost." He brought Jamie out from behind him.

Jamie uttered a little cry and threw himself against his father's legs, wrapping his arms tightly around them.

"What—?" Robert started to say when the man smiled.

"I said no questions," he repeated, then he was gone.

Anne stared after him, stunned. He had looked vaguely familiar. Then the thought fled on the heels of another: Jamie was back. He was safe!

Robert pried his son's arms from around his legs and bent to lift him into his arms. He was wearing only a swimsuit but he had no bruises that he could see, no cuts. He looked at the dear little face, inscribing it indelibly on his mind. Then, giving an inarticulate cry he crushed the boy against him. Jamie held tightly in return. When he opened his eyes he saw Anne, and he reached out to her, including her in their tiny group.

Anne went willingly, laughing and crying at the same time. She was so happy that he was back. So happy!

Chapter Twelve

Happiness is a capricious emotion, there one moment . . . gone the next.

Anne and Robert rejoiced in Jamie's return, but all too soon, reality reasserted itself and they had to know what had happened to him.

Jamie excitedly told them. Buoyed by the turn of events, the entire affair seemed a big adventure to him.

"A man grabbed me by the swimming pool. I didn't think you'd mind if I went swimming. You were sleeping, and—"

"Tell us what happened," Robert instructed, cutting into his son's litany of justification.

Jamie nodded. "He took me to his car and then to a house. Only we didn't stay there long. He put me in the car again and we went to a big building with a basement. He made me sit in a corner."

"The man who brought you here?" Robert prompted.

Jamie shook his head vigorously. "No—that man came later."

"What did the first man look like?" Anne asked.

"He was tall. He had funny kinda hair. It was short and stood up."

Anne nodded at Robert, wordlessly telling him that the description could fit Randall Elliot.

"Go on, sport," Robert said.

Jamie took another breath. "Well...we stayed there for a while. I asked him for some water, but he wouldn't give me any. He was acting kinda funny. He kept moving around and saying things to himself."

"What kind of things?"

Jamie shrugged. "I don't know."

"Then the other man came?" Robert prodded.

Again Jamie nodded. "He came bustin' through the door. The man with the funny hair jumped! Then he got all mad. He started yelling at the big man. I understood what he said that time, but I don't know..."

"What did he say?"

"He said something about money...about not paying him anything ever. He was really mad.

"The big man...he started yelling right back and he knocked over some boxes trying to get to him. The other man was running, trying to hide behind things. I think he was scared. Then the big man caught him."

Jamie became silent.

"What happened then?" Robert asked quietly.

"He hit him."

"What were you doing all this time?"

"I was in the corner, tryin' to stay out of the way."

"Smart boy," Robert approved, smiling at his son for the first time since his recitation started.

Jamie grinned back.

"What happened next?" Anne asked.

"The man hit him a lot. Then he threw him down and came for me. I tried to get away. I thought he was goin' to hit me, too. But he was real nice to me. He said he had a nephew my age." Jamie paused, wondering about the other boy before he continued, "Then he brought me here."

"And neither of the men hurt you?"

"No."

Robert hugged his son and closed his eyes, thanking whatever deity had watched over him for doing such a good job.

Jamie accepted the embrace before wiggling away. He grinned at Anne and then at his father. "I'm hungry! Could we get some hamburgers and potato chips?"

At that moment, Robert would have given his son anything he wanted. "Sure." Robert grinned at Anne. She understood perfectly what he was feeling. "I think Anne and I could use one, too. We haven't had anything to eat since lunch, either."

Jamie gave a little squeal.

"But first, I have to make a telephone call."

"'Kay."

"Anne, will you—"

Again Anne understood. She moved to Jamie's side and talked with him until Robert's return from the other room.

"Son, the person I called wants to see you. He wants to talk with you about what happened." To Anne, Robert continued, "Someone made an anonymous call...about where to find Randall Elliot. At first Elliot denied everything, then he broke down and confessed...about his involvement with the Kinkaid brothers, about hiring a man to kill you, about snatching Jamie. Made a clean breast of it. The deputy said he's not a pretty sight—that someone really did a job on him. Elliot blames the hit man—gave him his description." Robert paused, bemused. "I think it was the man who brought Jamie back here."

Anne immediately stiffened. "That's where I saw him before! He's the one who tried to run us off the road!"

Robert shook his head. "Well, he certainly did us a favor tonight."

Anne still couldn't believe everything that had happened.

"He was a nice man," Jamie piped up. "He told me all about his nephew."

Robert and Anne looked at each other. The ways of the world were certainly mysterious.

JAMIE HAD HIS BURGER and his chips—as many chips as he wanted. Then they went to the sheriff's office to talk to the deputy.

Henry Wynstock was there along with a few other men and women. They were all sprawled about the room, some in chairs, some not . . . waiting for their arrival.

Anne recognized each of them, but she smiled only at Henry. He gave a slow smile in return.

"Glad you got your boy back," he murmured.

Anne didn't deny that Jamie was close to her. She wasn't his mother, but no mother could have been happier at his safe return than she.

"Thank you, Henry."

He indicated the people around him. "We've been looking for him."

Anne solemnly took in the other faces. A few of them had been part of the mob in front of the motel. Those people looked away, ashamed of their part in what had occurred. The others held her gaze. "Thank you," she said, acknowledging their contribution.

Henry nodded. "People here aren't so bad."

Anne couldn't give an answer. That was easy for him to say. He hadn't been the one to suffer at their hands.

"When things calm down a bit, I've got something to tell you," Henry leaned close to impart as the people roused themselves to file from the office. Robert and Jamie were talking with the deputy. "Give me a call tomorrow or the next day."

Anne suddenly remembered Jamie's mother. With the joy of his return, she had forgotten. She wondered if Robert had forgotten, too. How were they going to tell the boy? When would they tell him?

Henry looked at her closely. "What is it?" he asked, sensing her hesitation.

Anne glanced at the boy. He was sitting on the deputy's desk, motioning animatedly as he talked. He wouldn't be able to hear. "We just got word that Jamie's mother died today. We—I don't know what we're going to do...how long we're going to stay here."

Henry looked at her with compassion. "Things haven't been working out too good for you, have they? But I have a feeling they're going to change." He took a deep breath. "All right, I'll tell you now. This is something I've been planning on telling everyone . . . sooner or later. I'll just make it sooner in your case. I was the one who left those papers in your shop. I knew what was going on. I'd known for several weeks.

"I couldn't do anything about it myself. My pension was coming up and... And I couldn't face all the anger. So I took the easy way out and smuggled the papers into your shop. I knew you'd find them, and I knew what you'd do with them.

"I wanted to tell the people when everything blew up like it did. I didn't expect it to get that bad. But, I just couldn't do it. Not then. My pension was hanging in the balance. I wasn't sure if I'd get it or not since the company was going belly-up. And the people making the decision sure wouldn't look on me favorably if they knew what I'd done.

"And I needed that pension."

Anne said nothing.

"These have probably been the worst days of my life, knowing what I'd done to you. Then just now, I found out that Randall Elliot was involved, too. That he was one of the go-betweens. Contacting people, arranging things—for a handsome cut. I couldn't believe it. I also couldn't believe that he was desperate enough to do what he did to you. What he did to the boy." He dropped his balding head. "I have a lot to answer for."

Anne stirred. She was so very tired. What she wanted was an end to it all. A final end. She placed her hand lightly on Henry's arm, offering forgiveness, the only gift that would see it ended. "It's all over now," she said quietly. "Everything's done. I think what would be best for everyone is to try to forget it."

"I can't forget it," he contradicted. "I'll never be able to forget it."

Anne's hand fell away. She didn't know what more she could say to him.

Robert and Jamie stepped to her side. Jamie's eyes were shining from telling his tale of adventure again. Robert's face mirrored her own exhaustion. And a certain dullness in the blue of his eyes told her that he hadn't forgotten Jamie's mother or the ordeal they had yet to face.

"Let's get out of here," he murmured.

Anne nodded, turning away from Henry.

Before they got to the door, though, Henry called, "Keep in touch, Anne. Don't be a stranger."

It was an expression that one friend might use to another. But Anne couldn't face it right now. Instead of answering, she gave a halting wave, letting Henry read into it what he wished.

ROBERT DECIDED not to tell Jamie about his mother until the next morning. The boy had been through enough for one night. Another day wouldn't hurt.

However, the delay was difficult. Robert wrestled with the prospect for most of the night and woke up to it the next morning.

Jamie was in high spirits when he awakened, still excited by his adventure. He bounced on his wide bed, telling Robert once again about the big man and the bad man...and how nice the big man had been to him. He had liked the sheriff's deputy, too, he confided.

Robert nodded noncommittally, listening to his son's rushed words, hearing his bright laughter...knowing that soon he was going to have to crush that exuberant joy in life.

"Do you think Anne's awake?" Jamie asked, bouncing yet again on the bed.

Robert moved to sit at his son's side, stilling the child's active body.

"I don't know. Probably not. We had a hard day yesterday."

"Because you were worried about me?" Jamie asked, curious.

"Yes."

"You were worried?"

"Wouldn't you think we would be?"

Jamie thought for a moment and then nodded. "But it wasn't my fault. The bad man grabbed me. I yelled, but I couldn't get away."

"I don't blame you, Jamie."

Jamie cocked his head. He sensed something in his father's tone...a seriousness underlying the softness of his voice.

"Then why are you...?" He stopped, unable to frame the proper words.

"Why am I what?" Robert prompted. He knew he was delaying yet again, but it was so hard. He knew how intensely Jamie was going to take the news. The boy loved his mother with everything that was in him.

Jamie shrugged his thin shoulders.

Robert placed his hand on his son's back and began to rub the flesh between the small shoulder blades.

"I'm afraid we've had some bad news, sport."

Jamie looked up at his father, seeing the graveness of his expression. "What?" he asked, suddenly afraid again. Yesterday, he had been afraid, before coming home. Today, he had thought that was all over. He didn't like being afraid. It made him feel all tingly inside. But not a nice kind of tingly.

Robert raked a hand through his hair. He had seen the fear flash back into his son's eyes. The skin felt stretched across his face. His expression felt frozen, just as his soul did at that moment. Once he had wondered if he had a soul; now he knew that he did, because it was bleeding.

"It's about your mother," he managed, hearing his voice waver even as he tried to keep it steady.

"What about her?" Jamie asked.

Robert took a breath. "You know she was having a hard time with the baby..."

Jamie nodded.

"Well, she went into labor...to have the baby...to let it be born. And something happened."

Jamie's body was tense. Earlier he had been a spring, bouncing into the sky and then back onto the bed. Now he was just a spring, with nowhere to bounce.

"Somethin' happened to the baby?" he asked.

Robert nodded.

"Did it die?" Jamie whispered.

Again Robert nodded.

Jamie bit his bottom lip. He had been looking forward to having a little brother or sister...but a brother most of all.

"Why'd it die?" he asked at last.

Robert shook his head. He didn't know.

"Was it a boy?" Jamie asked again.

Once again, Robert couldn't tell him. "I didn't take the message. I was out looking for you. Anne talked with Bryce when he called."

Jamie instantly tried to jump to his feet. If Anne knew, he would go ask her. But his father stopped him before he could get entirely off the bed. His large hands helped settle him back onto the cover. Jamie looked at him in confusion.

"That's not all, Jamie," Robert said quietly, a hollow dread to his voice.

Jamie became very still.

"Your mother... Your mother didn't..." Robert's words broke. This was the hardest thing he had ever had to do in his life. How did a person tell another person that someone they loved was no longer alive? How did a father tell that to his son...especially when it was his son's mother who was dead and the child was barely old enough to understand?

Jamie shivered as a cold breeze trickled down his neck. He knew about death. He'd had a dog once that had run into the street when a big red car was coming. He had seen the dog get hit. Bryce had told him it was his fault...that he should have kept hold of Lucky...that if he had, the dog would still be all right.

He took a shaken breath. Was his mother dead? Was that what his father was trying to tell him?

His bottom lip started to quiver. "M—mommy died, too?" he asked, his eyes pleading with his father to deny it.

Robert's face twisted with pain. "Yes, sport. She did."

The trembling spread from Jamie's bottom lip to the rest of his body. His mommy? Dead? "No—" he moaned.

Robert reached out to enclose his son in his arms. The child felt so small, so vulnerable. "I'm afraid so, honey. Things like this just happen sometime. We don't know why." Robert cursed himself for sounding so ineffectual.

"But not Mommy!" Jamie denied it, fighting to speak through the tears that clogged his throat and that were also rushing into his eyes.

"I'm sure there wasn't anything anyone could do."

"Maybe I could have—"

"No!" Robert crushed the ravaged little face to his chest. Warm dampness seeped through his shirt to his skin. "You couldn't have done anything, Jamie. You didn't *do* anything." Robert knew the tendency his son had to blame himself. He had to be sure that the child didn't blame himself for this.

"But when I talked to her..."

"She told you how much she loved you. How much she wanted you back."

Jamie freed a hand to rub the knuckles against one closed eye.

"Just remember that, Jamie. Remember that forever. She loved you; she wanted you back."

As Jamie drew a halting breath, his arms snaked around his father's waist and hugged tight to his solid form. He began to cry softly, broken-heartedly.

Robert held the child against him, rocking slowly back and forth on the bed, infrequently making a soft unintelligible sound in answer to his son's inarticulate murmurings.

ANNE HAD BEEN WAITING anxiously in the next room for what had to be an hour. She had heard Jamie's excited voice when he awakened, and she had heard Robert's much deeper-voiced replies. Then nothing.

She had continued to wait, feeling that the moment was private, between father and son. Finally, when she heard what could only be a soft crying, she stepped to the door to open it silently.

Jamie was in his father's arms, his small body clinging to his strength. Robert's expression was one of shared pain. Neither of them heard her intrusion.

Quietly, she closed the door again and sat down on her bed to continue her vigil.

THE FUNERAL WAS a terrible experience. Jamie was distressed, Robert was stoic and suffering with his son, and Anne... Anne felt the emotions of everyone.

She didn't know Karen, other than what she had learned from Robert and Jamie. Her only vision of her as a person was in the picture she had seen. But she had insisted upon traveling with them to the suburb near San Francisco where Karen and her husband lived because Robert had been with her in her time of need. Robert had not protested more than once and later seemed glad of her presence.

She met Bryce Jennings and had her suspicions confirmed: he was a thoroughly unlikable man. Selfish, argumentative, and he didn't like Jamie at all. He barely noticed that the boy was there, taking on the role of chief mourner with a relish that was almost repulsive.

Directly after the funeral, he found Robert and told them he wanted Jamie's things out of his house before the day was over.

Anne had to restrain Robert from hitting him. Not that she didn't think he deserved it, but the day was already unsettling enough for Jamie. He didn't need more upset.

THEY RETURNED TO the cottage in Seal Cove. There were still a few days left on Robert and Jamie's rental and it was the only place Robert could think of to go. Anne helped them to settle in before returning to her own beach house.

Parting from them was difficult. She had been in their company for days, sharing their lives, letting them share hers. Now she felt as if a part of her was being cut off. She wouldn't be whole any longer. But she could think of no excuse to remain.

The familiarity of the beach house reproached her as she moved listlessly from one room to the next. Nothing had changed; *everything* had changed. She was no longer the same person who had come here looking for a place to hide, a place to heal. And yet everything that she had been through had made no effect on the inanimate house. It was still the same, as if it would be the same forever.

She sank down on the living room couch.

She wondered what they were doing now. Jamie had been so quiet. So had Robert. In other circumstances she might have felt like an intruder, but that wasn't the impression they gave. She had been accepted unconditionally into their unit. However, neither had tried to stop her when she unwillingly mentioned that she should leave.

Anne dropped her face into her hands. She loved him. She loved him more than she thought it was possible to love anyone. And she loved his son. He could have been hers, she loved him that much. They had been through so much together.

Was it all going to end?

Was the world going to turn on its axis yet again, just as it had for millions of years, witnessing the joys and heartbreaks of its inhabitants, but unable to do anything except turn? This time, would it watch as her life, Robert's and Jamie's continued to shatter into lonely little bits?

Anne's body shook as she murmured Robert's name.

JAMIE WALKED ACROSS the sandy beach, indifferent to the cries of the sea birds, indifferent to the interesting bits and pieces of flotsam that a short week before would have intrigued him. His father was at his side. Jamie drew comfort from his presence. He needed him there, rock-steady, never changing . . . loving him. His hand was held loosely and yet comfortingly tight in his father's much larger one.

They came to a piece of driftwood that had washed ashore and was the size and length of a tree trunk. It had been sitting in the sun for a long time, drying out, its top surface smooth.

Robert sat down and Jamie followed suit.

For a long time they sat staring out to sea. Then Robert said quietly. "It's okay to cry, you know."

"I know." Jamie hadn't cried since learning of his mother's death. All through the ceremony of the funeral, his eyes had been big and watery but no tears had fallen.

"I know you're going to miss her...that you *do* miss her."

Jamie nodded.

"I'm sorry I didn't get you back in time to see her again."

"My baby brother died, too. I heard Bryce telling someone about his son. I knew he wasn't talkin' about me."

"No."

Jamie fidgeted. "I miss Anne. Why'd she go back to the other house?"

"I believe she thought we might like to be alone."

"I love her! I don't want her to go away, too!"

Robert hesitated before he spoke. He wasn't sure how much Jamie was capable of accepting at the moment. But from the tears he saw glistening in the boy's eyes, he decided to be honest. "I love her, too."

Jamie sniffed. "Then why can't she stay with us?"

"Things aren't always as simple as people want them to be, Jamie. Anne might need a little time to think. A lot has happened in her life recently."

"You mean like the man who wanted to hurt her?"

Robert nodded.

"I didn't like him."

"You don't ever have to worry about him again."

"Is he in jail?" Jamie asked, a spark of curiosity relighting in his eyes.

"Yes. And he will be for a long, long time."

"He won't be able to hurt Anne again?"

"No."

"I still want her to stay with us."

Robert smiled slowly. "I do, too."

"Then let's tell her!" Slowly, Jamie was emerging from his state of mourning. It didn't take children long to resume their lives. Not that he loved his mother any less...not that there wouldn't be times when he would cry for her. He was just ready to move on to the next subject at hand.

"This is something I don't think we should rush. Anne may not want to live with us."

"You gonna ask her to marry you, right?"

"I've thought about it."

"Then...that's it!" Jamie was shrugging his shoulders. He looked as if a minor earthquake was rocking him.

Robert tousled his hair. "Let's give it until tomorrow, sport. Okay?"

"Why?" the boy demanded.

"Because I think it would be best. Trust me?"

Jamie nodded and Robert laid an arm around his son's shoulders. How could he explain that he couldn't ask another woman to marry him on the same day as his first wife's funeral? Even if he had never loved Karen, there had been something between them...once. Enough to produce the child who was sitting so close to him. He owed her that much respect.

Robert transferred his gaze back to the sea. He had done some growing up over the past few weeks. Before he had been unsure, but he now knew where he was going...at least on the emotional level. He knew more about being a father, about how difficult it was, as well as how rewarding. He now knew that he would never be able to tell Jamie that he would never let anything hurt him...things like that were out of his power. He would love him, he would protect him, he would give unconditionally of himself. That was all any parent could do.

He also had come to a reconciliation with the memory of his own father. He understood the man better now—his faults as well as his good points.

Once he had heard that a child never understands his parents until he becomes a parent himself. He hadn't thought the message was for him, but the age-old wisdom held true.

For a time he had met every challenge, played every game, in rebellion against the kind of "nowhere" life he thought his father had led. Then he had come to the point of hollowness where he had ached for meaning in his life . . . for purpose.

Now he saw that if his father's life had held nothing else, it had held purpose. He'd had a family that he loved and that he was doing everything he could to care for.

Luckily, Robert had Jamie, and the boy had reached out to him in love. And now he had found Anne.

They gave to him much more than he ever would be able to repay.

Jamie heaved a great sigh, tucking his head against his father's shoulder.

A short time later, Robert noticed the stillness of his son's small body and bent to carry him back to the cottage.

Once he put the boy to bed, he stood just outside the door, wanting to be as impulsive as his child. But he held himself in check.

Tomorrow. He would wait for tomorrow, with the hope that there would be many more tomorrows to come.

Chapter Thirteen

Anne was resting on the chaise longue on the deck. Earlier she had cleaned the beach house from one end to the other, just to have something to do. Still, it was barely ten o'clock in the morning. The rest of the long day faced her. She didn't know how she was going to get through the hours that remained.

She wanted to go over to the cottage. She wanted to see them, she missed them so. But she wouldn't let herself.

Once Robert had said something about love. About loving her. She remembered the words, and yet she didn't. Was it that she had wanted to hear him say it? Had she wanted it so badly that she hallucinated? Or had he said them and then immediately regretted it?

Everything had been so out of kilter. Their lives had been turned upside down. Intimacies were accepted as normalcy. They had kissed, they had held each other... Did that mean anything now?

Anne shivered in the warmth. She needed him, she wanted him, she loved him. But possibly she was the type of person who would never receive love in return. Through no fault of her own, was she meant to be solitary? From childhood on, was she never destined to find the hidden treasures of love and warmth and caring?

Anne groaned as she hid her eyes from the sun, crooking her arm over the upper portion of her face.

Then she heard a sound . . . a muffled childish giggle. Immediately her heart leapt. Jamie? And if it was Jamie, would Robert be with him?

She sat up, trying to adjust her vision to the brightness of day, trying to see into the distance. She stepped to the railing but was careful not to lean against it. She would never lean against a railing again.

Almost at once, she saw two blond heads emerge along the embankment. Robert was carrying his son on his shoulders. Jamie looked up and saw her. He cried her name and waved.

Anne swallowed the tightness in her throat even as her eyes drank in the vision of the two people she loved most in the world. Her hand trembled as she returned the wave.

Robert looked up at that moment and she met the electric-blue gaze. For several seconds he didn't move . . . then he crossed the fence, leaning over to put Jamie on his own feet.

Jamie immediately ran the distance to the stairs and clambered up them. He threw himself into Anne's arms, his thin arms strong as they held her tightly.

Anne held him just as tightly back. She closed her eyes, drinking up the feel of the child, thanking God for this moment.

She heard a heavier footstep on the wooden deck and her eyes instantly opened. Robert was standing there, looking at her. Her gaze went over his face, searching out the remembered features, aware of his handsomeness even as she was aware of his essence.

Jamie pulled away. He had been warned not to say anything concerning what he and his father had talked about last evening...to let Robert handle the situation. But the words popped out before he could stop them. "Anne...we want you to marry us!" Then he looked at his father, his face stricken with what he had done.

Robert gave a soft grunt, shaking his head with mock reproach.

Jamie squeezed Anne's hand. "I wasn't supposed to say that," he whispered. "I was supposed to let Daddy—"

"Don't you think that's enough, sport? When do I get my turn?"

Anne's mouth felt stiff. Her entire body felt stiff. Yet what she needed to do most of all was sit down.

Robert saw the way Anne was holding herself, the frozen look on her face and suddenly he felt unsure. Last night it had seemed so simple: come over to the beach house, talk to her, tell her how his feelings for her had grown. He hadn't considered for a moment that she might reject his words. Robert shifted uneasily.

Jamie looked from one adult to the other. He didn't understand what the problem was.

Robert drew his son close, keeping his hands on his slim shoulders. He needed the moral support. "We, ah. I—"

Anne couldn't bear to listen to a disclaimer. Jamie had things confused. Now Robert was trying to find a way out. She forced a smile and asked brightly,

"Would you like something to drink? I made some tea earlier. It should be cold by now. I'll go get it." She escaped into the house.

Jamie watched her quick exit and turned to his father. "What's the matter with Anne?" he asked.

Robert took a deep breath and bent low to answer his son. "Sometimes people need to go slow. Do you understand that? They have to—" he paused, trying to think of the correct wording "—they have to feel their way. Anne and I have to do that now."

"But why?" Jamie demanded. "She likes us and we like her. We like her a lot!"

Robert raked a hand through his hair, trying to find the best way to explain. "Yes, we do. And I do think Anne likes us. But...we can't take anything for granted. Maybe she likes us, but not enough to marry us. Not enough to live with us. Can you understand that?"

Some of the brightness left Jamie's face. Once again, it became old beyond his years. "And you have to find out real slow, huh?"

Robert nodded.

Jamie sighed. "Would it be okay if I go for a swim?"

Robert put a finger under his son's chin and lifted it from where it had fallen. "You go for a swim and I'll try to convince Anne. Deal?"

A smile flickered on Jamie's mouth. "Deal."

He shucked his shorts and shirt, and jumped down the steps in the swim trunks he wore beneath. He had put them on, just in case.

Robert smiled as he folded the articles of clothing and placed them on the small, round table beside the chaise longue.

Anne stepped outside at that point, carrying a tray with three glasses. Her face was arranged, not showing the tumult that was going on inside her. She felt as if she were at the end of the known world. One step more and she would fall into an abyss that could be filled either with happiness or with despair.

Her glance slid over Robert, her heart quickening its pace as a result.

Robert stepped close to take the tray, accidentally touching one of her hands. It was as cold as ice.

"Jamie decided to go for a swim. That's all right, isn't it?" he asked.

Anne nodded. "Yes. It's fine."

He put the tray on the table, pushing the clothes over a bit, then he took one of the glasses and handed it to her.

Anne accepted it but wished that she hadn't. She didn't want anything to drink.

He lifted a glass for himself and drank thirstily. Anne watched his throat move; it was an intimate action. She quickly looked away.

When he lowered the glass, his eyes settled on her and he cleared his throat. He couldn't believe he was as nervous as he was. Him? Who had never been nervous around a woman before! But he had never faced a moment like this before—one that would influence the rest of his life as well as his son's. He searched his mind for the right thing to say. All he could come up with was, "Jamie's better today."

"I could see that."

"He—ah—he got better last night. He still misses his mother, though."

"I'm sure he does."

She wasn't helping. Robert tried again. "Children heal quickly."

Anne walked to the railing. She put the glass on its level surface but kept her fingers entwined around it. "Not always, they don't."

Robert came close to her side, drawn to her but not yet able to reach out and touch her. He kept his distance. "You sound like you know what you're talking about." He wanted to keep her talking. When she gave those quick, flat answers, it unnerved him even more.

"I do." She paused. Jamie was splashing about in the pool below. She kept her eyes on him even though she was looking into the past. "Sometimes hurts keep on hurting. Sometimes you can't get away from them. Jamie will . . . because he has you."

"You think I make that much difference to him?"

"Don't you?"

Robert took the glass from her hands and placed it on the table alongside his. Then he turned her slowly to face him. "Could I make that much difference to you?" His words were soft, husky.

Anne closed her eyes. How did she answer without overwhelming him? He was the day, the night, the moon and the stars to her. He was everything. And his son would merely complete her happiness. Did she answer truthfully, or did she hedge, trying to keep some small smattering of dignity? But after everything that had happened in Overton, after having opened herself completely to him already, she didn't have any false dignity left. She countered with another question, playing for time. "Would you want to?"

"The pain you felt in Overton will go away, Anne. It won't stay with you forever."

Anne said nothing. She just continued to look at him with those great golden eyes. She hadn't been thinking of Overton. She had been thinking of her childhood, and how the coldness of her father had stayed with her throughout the years. That kind of pain didn't go away. Jamie's would, because he had the love of both his mother, before she died, and his father. She? She had no one. Unless...

"Would you want to?" she repeated at last, her voice barely audible.

Robert's hands tightened on her arms. He was having the most difficult time restraining himself. "Would you want me to?" he countered.

Two people... both hurt by the world around them and by the worlds of their own making.

"What are you saying, Robert?"

Her tight question was all that Robert could stand. He didn't care anymore if she would feel rushed. If she would resent his precipitous action. He pulled her toward him, needing her more than he had ever needed anyone before in his life.

When he bent to kiss her, Anne met his need with her own, her arms wrapping around his back, pulling him closer, pulling herself closer to him. Into her kiss she poured all the feelings in her heart: love, because that was her main emotion; fear, because she was afraid ever to lose him; desire, because she wanted him above everything else; and certainty—because even if this was a moment out of time and didn't mean anything to the future, it did to her. It meant everything to her.

She had no home in the physical sense. Nowhere in the world could she feel secure. But in Robert— In Robert lay the security, the caring, the warmth that she had always longed for. In him, in his spirit, was her sense of place. Wherever he went, she would go—even if they parted in the next hour.

Robert didn't question what would happen in the future. He didn't dare let himself speculate on anything beyond what was occurring at that second. Anne was in his arms—he was holding her! touching her!—and she was responding, touching him in return . . . as if she couldn't get enough of him.

Robert was the first to pull away. Suddenly he had to be sure that he wasn't dreaming. He looked at Anne, at the star-burst quality in her eyes. And in them, he saw the answer he had been searching for most of his life, without really knowing that he was looking.

In her, he had found the answer to the eternal puzzle. With her, he would never be alone again. Because of her, he became a complete human being, capable of all the joy, all the ecstasy, all the rewards received when he shared himself completely.

He cradled her face in hands that were not quite steady. She looked back at him, waiting for him to speak.

He cleared his throat. "What Jamie said . . . What he said when we first came. I . . ." He could get no farther.

Anne smiled. She turned her head to kiss the inside of his wrist. Robert was one of the strongest people she had ever known—in himself, in how he perceived himself. He had made mistakes. He didn't try to deny any of them. But his worst mistake was the one he was trying hardest to rectify. He was a good father, and one day Jamie would tell him so.

And her? Because of Robert she had learned never to hide—from the world or from herself. She was ready to face almost anything now, except the prospect of losing him, of losing his son.

But that wasn't going to happen now. That possibility was receding with each second that passed. To hurry it along, Anne answered softly, "The answer's yes . . . if you want me."

Robert momentarily closed his eyes. If he wanted her! He didn't answer verbally; he let his body do his talking.

Damp fingers touched Anne's elbow and she jumped, startled.

Robert's breathing was heavy as he slowly loosened her and looked down at his son's expectant face.

Beads of water still glistened on the child's skin and matted down his hair, but the grin that spread from ear to ear could not be inhibited by the water pooling at his feet.

"Does this mean she's gonna marry us?" he asked his father, waiting for the right word to show his excitement.

Anne slipped out of Robert's arms and knelt to speak to his son. "Are you sure you want me to, Jamie?"

"Course! You can be my new mommy. Not my real mommy . . . but my new mommy!"

Anne bent forward to hug him. "I'll try to be a good one. I promise."

Jamie grinned again. "Course!" It was his favorite new word. Then he gave a whoop of happiness and scooted down the stairs to take a flying leap into the pool. Water splashed everywhere and he came up laughing at his feat.

Robert held his arm around Anne's waist as they watched the boy. "Are you sure you're ready to take us on?" he asked humorously.

"Course," she mimicked.

He kissed the tip of her nose.

"Would you mind living in India for a time?"

"India?" she repeated, surprised.

He nodded. "I have about six months left on my commitment. I think you and Jamie will love it. I can show you all the wonderful places . . . and you should see the reverse side, too. No one should just see one face to a country. You have to see it as a whole to understand it . . . to really love it."

"As you do."

He conceded. "As I do."

"Would six months be long enough?"

"You'd be willing to stay longer?"

"If I'm with you."

Robert had never known such unselfish caring. He smoothed her hair with his hand, telling her without words of his love.

"I think six months is enough. We can come back to the States . . . settle down. Find a place for Jamie to go to school."

"Where?"

Robert shrugged. "Who knows? Do you have a suggestion?"

"What about your job? Don't you want to—"

"I've had a long-standing offer to write a column for a news-magazine back east. I think I might take them up on it."

"Would you enjoy doing that?"

"I've thought about it a lot lately. I want to do it. And not just because of you, or Jamie. I think I might have something to say."

Anne dropped her head to his shoulder. "When do you have to go back to India?"

"In two weeks. India is a wonderful place for a honeymoon."

Anne gave a little smile. "Do I get a real proposal first?"

"I thought you had."

Anne shook her head. "No, Jamie proposed for you."

"Well, since he's going to be in on the honeymoon..."

"I don't mind...not at all. I love Jamie."

"Speaking of which, I still haven't heard you actually say the magic words."

Anne's smile grew. She shook her head. "Not until I get a proposal."

Robert laughed outright, hugging her close. "All right—*Anne*!" he said loudly, for anyone to hear. Jamie even looked up from the pool. *"Will you marry me?"*

Jamie jumped up and down.

Anne joined in with their spirit of fun. *"Yes!"* she called to the world. "And I love you," she said much more softly... only to Robert.

He barely breathed her name as he pulled her close to his heart.

Neither of them heard the triumphant whoop Jamie gave, nor saw the near-perfect dive he made into the crisp, clear water of the pool, where their lives had crossed and held on a similar cloudless day several weeks before.

Epilogue

Anne's body automatically stiffened as landmarks became more familiar.

Robert sensed her unease and pressed her hand against his thigh. "We don't have to do this," he said, keeping his eyes on the curving road ahead.

"Henry would be disappointed if we don't."

Throughout their months in India, she and Henry Wynstock had exchanged several letters. Anne had been the first to write—originally, to reassure him that she held no ill feelings toward him for what he had done, and also to help her complete the task of putting that difficult time totally behind her. She now had a new life. She had no need to harbor grudges. And, if things hadn't happened just as they did, she would never have met Robert and Jamie. She would have been content to stay in Overton, living quietly and alone...

Jamie looked up from the comic book he was reading. During their time in India, he had tanned almost as darkly as his father. He had loved the country and its people, making friends wherever he went. But most importantly, he had lost the sense of quiet desperation that had plagued him during his earlier years. He was more confident, less easy to feel at fault. "Are we almost there?" he asked.

Anne nodded, her gaze sweeping lovingly over the boy. He grinned at her, the feeling mutual.

"Do you think they're gonna like us this time?"

"I have no idea. Henry just asked that we stop by when we came back."

They had been in the United States for two weeks now, living at the beach house—an extension of their honeymoon, Robert had teased.

To Anne, it all still seemed like a dream: their marriage...their move to such an exotic land as India...and now the move back to California. Sometimes she was afraid that she would wake up and find that none of it was true—that she was still afraid of every tiny noise that sounded.

Her hand moved on her husband's thigh, reassuring herself that he was real. She felt him stir and steal a quick glance. She met his look with a small, satisfied smile.

Living with Robert had been a revelation. He was the exact opposite of her father. His warmth, his love, his gentleness had only grown with each day that passed. And his sense of fun made existence wonderful. She could feel herself flowering in his care, in his passion.

When she had broached the idea of returning to Overton for a visit, he had listened without interruption and agreed without protest. If that was what she wanted to do, it was all right with him.

Now, she wasn't as sure.

Henry had asked them to meet him at the gazebo. Anne had thought that odd but agreed.

When they pulled up to the tree-lined square, Robert was the first to spot him. Henry was leaning against one of the supporting white posts and when he saw them start to get out of the car, he pushed off to greet them.

He shook hands solemnly with Robert and Jamie and saved a warm hug for Anne at the last.

"You look like life's treating you better, young lady," he said.

Anne smiled in return to his greeting. "It is."

"Good...good...glad to hear that."

Anne glanced around the square, remembering the last time she had been there. Remembering Randall Elliot.

"I'm also glad you agreed to come back by." Henry's voice broke into her thoughts. "There's something I want to show you. Come on...it's over here."

He started to moved away and Anne, Robert and Jamie followed, exchanging puzzled looks.

When she saw that he was leading them toward her print shop, Anne's footsteps started to lag. She still had done nothing about the mess within. She and Robert had talked it over and decided that when they returned to the States, they would deal with the problem. But she didn't want to see it again. Not now. Not—

Henry didn't stop outside the shop. He produced a key and put it to the lock. When the door swung open, he motioned for Anne to step inside first.

Anne hesitated, then did as he directed, bracing herself for what was to come. She didn't understand why Henry was doing this! She reached for Robert's hand as he followed her inside.

Then to her surprise, she stared at the cleaned-up room. Gone were the broken pieces of copy machines, of printers, of destroyed supplies. In their place sat replacements, all clean and new and ready for use.

Anne smoothed a hand down one of the machines, her disbelieving eyes turning on Henry. "Who—?" she whispered, unable to voice more thoughts.

"It's yours...every bit of it. Everyone chipped in."

"But the insurance—"

"That's all taken care of. The insurance company is holding the check for you."

"But—" Anne started to say when Henry interrupted.

"That's not all. Come on...let's get in your car and go to your house."

Anne let herself be led from the shop and across the street to the car. Henry sat in the back seat with Jamie and kept up a teasing conversation with the boy all the short distance to her house.

A number of other cars were parked along the sides of the street. Anne looked at them in confusion. She didn't understand.

Robert's hand was at her back, urging her forward, as they walked up the pathway. She looked around at him and saw his wink. Jamie had come up to take her hand. He was grinning happily, too.

Henry Wynstock paused at the door, but only to give one sharp knock before opening it.

The house seemed full of people. Anne saw all the faces but also saw beyond. Just as she had discovered at the shop, the house had been cleaned and re-painted and her furniture had been restored.

All the faces waited for her to speak. She felt the pressure but didn't know what to say.

Henry Wynstock stepped forward. "Anne...we want to apologize to you. For everything we did, for what we said. We know that this can't make it all up to you, but—"

Several other voices joined in, expressing like sentiments.

The faces became a blur for Anne. She bit her bottom lip to keep it from trembling.

"We'd like you to think about coming back to Overton to live...you and your man and your boy," Henry continued. "Things still aren't the same as they were before the Kinkaids left, but they've steadied off. And people are coming around to the right way of thinking. They don't blame you anymore for what happened."

An uneasy silence followed. Anne knew that most of this had been Henry's work. He must have lobbied on her behalf for months.

"I don't know what to say," she murmured truthfully.

"Nothing's needed," he returned. He glanced at the men and women filling the room. "Dinner ready?"

"Dinner?" Anne echoed.

Henry smiled, "The least we can do is feed you."

Anne was swept into the general feeling of good will. People came up to her and to Robert and started to talk. Some children took Jamie outside to play.

Two hours later, they were back in the car.

"Did what I think happened really happen?" Anne asked, bemused as they started the drive back to the beach house.

Robert smiled broadly. "It happened."

"I can't believe it."

"Turn and wave to the people."

Anne turned around and saw that the people had clustered into her front yard. She waved as the car continued to pull away. They waved in return.

"They like you now," Jamie said, turning from waving as well.

"Yes."

"So what do you want to do?" Robert asked. "Come back here to live? Jamie and I are open to anything, aren't we, sport?"

Jamie nodded enthusiastically.

Still Anne frowned. "I don't know. I'll have to think about it." Then she lapsed into a silence that lasted most of the way back to the beach house.

ANNE CLOSED THE DOOR behind herself and Robert after they had tucked Jamie into bed for the night. Over the past months, they had worked out a satisfactory solution to his nap-taking and his bedtime. He didn't take naps anymore, but he went to bed earlier at night—which was perfect for Anne and Robert, giving them time to be alone.

They went outside on the deck, arm in arm, to stand in the moonlight. Robert tipped up her chin to kiss her long and satisfactorily.

Anne leaned the back of her head against his chest as she turned to face the water. His arms wrapped around her waist and her body tucked against his length.

This was how she wanted her life to continue.

Robert's breath stirred the hair beside her ear as he said softly, "This has been quite a day."

She agreed with a tiny shake of her head.

"Jamie enjoyed it," he continued.

Again she nodded.

"Did you?" he asked.

She was slow in answering. "I think I did."

He gave a soft laugh. "I know what you mean."

"It was very sweet of Henry."

"He still feels guilty."

"They all do."

"Have you given it any more thought? Do you want to live there again?"

Anne moved her fingers over his arm. She felt so safe and secure with him.

"I still don't know. In a way I wouldn't mind. But in another way..."

"It's too soon," he finished for her.

She nodded. "I think it is."

"Then we won't, at least not now. There are plenty of other places."

"But what will we do with the house...with the shop? After all the trouble they went to, I don't want to make them feel bad."

Robert marveled that she could be so sensitive to the feelings of the people who had been so hateful to her. But that was part of Anne—part of the woman he loved.

"I'm not being silly, you know," she said, turning to glance up at him. "They went to a lot of effort.

They're trying to make it up to us in the only way they know how. That's why I—"

He didn't let her finish. "That's why you're being such a marshmallow," he teased. Then he sobered. "But I understand. And I don't have a solution."

"Overton's not a bad place," she continued, murmuring her thoughts aloud. "At least there we'd know what we were letting ourselves in for. We'd know the people. And they'd know us." She paused. "And it wouldn't be an unacceptable place for Jamie to grow up. It's small, the schools are good."

Robert nuzzled her hair. "Sounds like you're changing your mind."

Anne moved her cheek closer to his lips. "Maybe I am."

"Anywhere is fine with me . . . as long as I'm with you."

"Maybe we could help the town get back on its feet—"

"To hell with Overton right now," he breathed. "We'll talk about it tomorrow. Right now, I—"

His lips slid closer to her mouth and Anne twisted around to meet him.

Robert lifted her into his arms. Then he made his way back through the doorway and down the hall to the bedroom they now shared.

Everything was quiet from Jamie's room. The boy usually went to sleep fairly fast.

Now the moment was purely for Anne and himself. And he didn't want the past or the future to impinge upon it.

He laid her on the bed and stretched out beside her. His pale eyes glided over her, from the top of her beautiful chestnut hair to the small feet that had brought her to him.

In his mind, the entire process of their meeting had been miraculous. One misstep, one different move...one different agony...and they might have missed each other for eternity.

He felt Anne's body come alive beneath the touch of his hand.

Anne smoothed the shirt away from his chest, then from his shoulders, then dropped it to the floor.

She looked up into the very blue eyes and in them saw love and desire and devotion.

And she knew, if she hadn't known before, that she at last had found her home.

JOIN THE CELEBRATION!
THE FIFTH ANNIVERSARY
OF HARLEQUIN
AMERICAN ROMANCE

1988 is a banner year for Harlequin American Romance—it marks our fifth anniversary.

For five successful years we've been bringing you heartwarming, exciting romances, but we're not stopping there. In 1988 we've got an extraspecial treat for you. Join us next month when we feature four of American Romance's best—and four of your favorite—authors.

Judith Arnold, Rebecca Flanders, Beverly Sommers and Anne Stuart will enchant you with the stories of four women friends who lived in the same New York apartment building and whose lives, one by one, take an unexpected turn. Meet Abbie, Jaime, Suzanne and Marielle—the women of YORKTOWN TOWERS.

Look for . . .

#257 SEARCH THE HEAVENS by Rebecca Flanders

Jaime Faber didn't believe in bucking the system. Unlike her flamboyant mother, she lived conservatively, with no surprises. Until her social work took her to Victory House, in the ethnic heart of New Orleans. Jaime didn't know which threatened her more—the curse put on her by a voodoo queen, or the unpredictable, free-spirited Dr. Quaid Gerreau.

#258 REACH FOR THE SKY by Beverly Sommers

Suzanne Allman had read all about the depressing empty-nest syndrome, but now that her daughter, Mouse, was leaving for college, Suzanne felt nothing but happiness. She could finally quit her high-paying acting job and start living life for herself. But driving Mouse cross-country brings Suzanne more than just freedom. It brings her handsome young Wyoming cowboy Billy Blue. Now that she's finally on her own, is Suzanne ready for love?

#259 HARVEST THE SUN by Judith Arnold

For Abbie Jarvis, life in the big city was worth every sacrifice. But when prosecuting an emotional case leaves her needing R and R, she retreats to her small northern California hometown. In need of a friend, she walks straight into the arms of T.J. Hillyard, local hero. Like T.J., Abbie had tasted the glory she yearned for—but was it enough? Or had what she'd been looking for always been right in her own backyard?

#260 CRY FOR THE MOON by Anne Stuart

Marielle Brandt didn't have much choice after she was suddenly widowed and left alone to raise her two small children. The only legacy from her husband was Farnum's Castle, a run-down apartment house in Chicago. The building housed some eccentric inhabitants, including two psychics and a warlock— but it also was home to Simon Zebriskie, resident helper and late-night DJ. It seemed to Marielle a most unlikely place to fall in love, but how could she deny Simon's powerful sensuality?

Four believable American Romance heroines . . . four contemporary American women just like you . . . by four of your favorite American Romance authors.

Don't miss these special stories. Enjoy the fifth-anniversary celebration of Harlequin American Romance.

★SPECIAL ANNIVERSARY ISSUE★
5 YEAR
★SPECIAL ANNIVERSARY ISSUE★

Lynda Ward's

LEAP THE MOON

... the continuing saga of *The Welles Family*

You've already met Elaine Welles, the oldest daughter of powerful tycoon Burton Welles, in Superromance #317, *Race the Sun*. You cheered her on as she threw off the shackles of her heritage and won the love of her life, Ruy de Areias.

Now it's her sister's turn. Jennie Welles is the drop-dead-gorgeous, most rebellious Welles sister, and she's determined to live life her way—and flaunt it in her father's face.

When she meets Griffin Stark, however, she learns there's more to life than glamour and independence. She learns about kindness, compassion and sharing. One nagging question remains: is she good enough for a man like Griffin? Her father certainly doesn't think so....

Leap the Moon ... a Harlequin Superromance coming to you in August. Don't miss it!